# The Midwife's Apprentice

# The Midwife's Apprentice

## Karen Cushman

🐦 sandpiper

Houghton Mifflin Harcourt
BOSTON NEW YORK

www.hmhco.com

The text of this book is set in 12/15-point Joanna.


The Library of Congress has cataloged the hardcover edition as follows:
Cushman, Karen.
The midwife's apprentice/by Karen Cushman.
p. cm.
Summary: In medieval England, a nameless, homeless girl is taken in by a sharp-tempered midwife and, in spite of obstacles and hardship, eventually gains the three things she most wants: a full belly, a contented heart, and a place in the world.
[1. Middle Ages—Fiction. 2. Midwives—Fiction.] I. Title.
Pz7.c962Mi 1995
[Fic]—dc20 94–13792
CIP
AC

ISBN: 978-0-395-69229-5 hardcover
ISBN: 978-0-547-72217-7 paperback

Printed in the United States of America
DOC 15 14 13 12 11

4500711852

For Philip and Dinah,
Alyce's midwives

# The Midwife's Apprentice

# AN INTRODUCTION

*The Midwife's Apprentice:* the title was in my head for a long time. I liked it, speaking as it did of birth and learning, but I didn't know what the story was about. The title was all I had. I wrote it on a card, put it in a folder marked "The Midwife's Apprentice," and filed it away, but I had no words to accompany it, and I despaired: Would it forever be an empty folder? Would I never know what I wanted to say? I sat at the computer and stared at the blank page. And then one day I saw an image of a homeless child sleeping on a dung heap, longing for a name, a full belly, and a place in the world, and the words flowed from my fingers. I finished a draft in record time and sent it to my editor, Dinah Stevenson, with a note saying, "I don't know if this is a novel or a writing exercise." Dinah thought it was indeed a novel, and *The Midwife's Apprentice* was published by Clarion Books in 1995.

Alyce, the midwife's apprentice, is alone and unsure but also courageous, compassionate, and resilient—a determined young woman in medieval England who finds her way in a world that's often brutal. But she is not feisty and outgoing like Birdy in *Catherine, Called Birdy,* and people love Birdy. Alyce is like the younger sister of the prom queen—would people appreciate her quieter charms?

I needn't have worried. *The Midwife's Apprentice* won the New-bery Medal in 1996, and my life has never been the same.

My husband once suggested that my third book, *The Ballad of Lucy Whipple*, told my own story of moving to California when I was ten. *Matilda Bone; The Loud Silence of Francine Green; Rodzina*, about a Polish girl from Chicago, like me; and *Alchemy and Meggy Swann*, with Meggy's wabbling and pain, are all my own stories. I cannot seem to write a book that isn't in some way about me. I told this to a group of seventh-graders while we were discussing *The Midwife's Apprentice*, and one boy, his grin full of glee, asked, "Does that mean you sleep on a dung heap?" No, I responded, but I, like Alyce, like all of us, was born longing for a name, a full belly, and place in the world. That didn't really satisfy him. He was hoping for the dung heap.

My novels often reflect the desire to be wanted or included, the need to find a place to belong. I am not surprised. Like Alyce and Meggy, Francine and Matilda, I was a bit of an outsider growing up, often lonely and confused, but stubborn and independent, trying to figure out the world and my place in it. I think we are all intrigued by the idea of who we are as individuals separate from our families and our homes. What would we do if we were on our own? How would we survive? Would we be resourceful and courageous, or helpless? Would we be the same people we are now, or would we grow to be different? What kind of family might we create for ourselves?

I wrote *The Midwife's Apprentice* in part because I wondered about these things, about courage and persistence, identity and responsibility, compassion and kindness and belonging. How could I know them if I didn't write about them?

Many reviewers have mentioned my "gutsy girls." I was not a "gutsy girl" growing up, and I never found models of such girls in the books available to me. But as we are what we eat and hear and experience, so too we are what we read. This, too, is why I write what I do, about gutsy girls—strong young women who in one way or another take responsibility for their own lives; about tolerance, thoughtfulness, and caring; about choosing what is life-affirming and generous; about the certainty of failure and the need for perseverance.

Of all my books, *The Midwife's Apprentice* has made most clear the important part readers as well as writers play in the creation of a book. Readers have asked me about the womb symbols, the numerous birth metaphors, and the significance of the number three in the book. What? Where? I am confounded—I did not consciously include any symbols or metaphors, but readers found them, and if I go back and reread, there they are. Once again, writer and reader are, as has been said, each on one side of the pencil.

At a signing, a five-year-old girl approached me. Her mother had just read the book to her and her two older sisters. "The book is all about a cat," the girl said. She told me what the cat did and said in this book, to her not about a midwife or her apprentice, but about a cat. And I told her that Lobelia, my own orange cat, sat on my lap while I wrote about Alyce and Purr, and sometimes she walked across the keyboard, adding her own words to mine.

The next year I received a letter from a high school English as a Second Language class, seniors from other countries—some homeless—who had read *The Midwife's Apprentice* and related to the story of a girl searching for a place in the world. They sent me a class photo. There they were, seventeen years old: girls with teased hair and eye makeup, six-foot-tall boys with mustaches, all holding up their copies of Alyce's story and smiling. They are all Alyce, seeking their name, their way, their place in this world so new to them.

How do I feel about *The Midwife's Apprentice* now, nearly twenty years later? I am proud of its simplicity and its wisdom. I often cite it as my favorite of my books because its creation gave me less trouble than my other titles. I love the character of Alyce—skinny, big-eyed, and hopeful—and the smart, independent, but tender Purr, an amalgam of all my beloved cats. And I still love what the book says about being in the world. My first draft ended with a despondent Alyce, having failed in a difficult delivery, leaving the midwife and the village to make a new life somewhere else. It soon became obvious that Alyce had to return to the village to confront her failure, to try again until she succeeds with courage, tenacity, and hope—as we all must. For Alyce's story is also my story, and your story, despite our not sleeping on a dung heap. I hope you enjoy it.

—*Karen Cushman*

# Contents

1. The Dung Heap                          1
2. The Cat                                6
3. The Midwife                           11
4. The Miller's Wife                     17
5. The Merchant                          25
6. The Naming                            33
7. The Devil                             40
8. The Twins                             48
9. The Bailiff's Wife's Baby             54
10. The Boy                              61
11. The Leaving                          67
12. The Inn                              72
13. Visitors                             82
14. The Manor                           89
15. Edward                              95
16. The Baby                           104
17. The Midwife's Apprentice           112
    Author's Note                      118

# 1.
# The Dung Heap

WHEN ANIMAL DROPPINGS and garbage and spoiled straw are piled up in a great heap, the rotting and moiling give forth heat. Usually no one gets close enough to notice because of the stench. But the girl noticed and, on that frosty night, burrowed deep into the warm, rotting muck, heedless of the smell. In any event, the dung heap probably smelled little worse than everything else in her life—the food scraps scavenged from kitchen yards, the stables and sties she slept in when she could, and her own unwashed, unnourished, unloved, and unlovely body.

How old she was was hard to say. She was small and pale, with the frightened air of an ill-used child, but her scrawny, underfed body did

1

give off a hint of woman, so perhaps she was twelve or thirteen. No one knew for sure, least of all the girl herself, who knew no home and no mother and no name but Brat and never had. Someone, she assumed, must have borne her and cared for her lest she toddle into the pond and changed her diapers when they reeked, but as long as she could remember, Brat had lived on her own by what means she could—stealing an onion here or helping with the harvest there in exchange for a night on the stable floor. She took what she could from a village and moved on before the villagers, with their rakes and sticks, drove her away. Snug cottages and warm bread and mothers who hugged their babes were beyond her imagining, but dearly would she have loved to eat a turnip without the mud of the field still on it or sleep in a barn fragrant with new hay and not the rank smell of pigs who fart when they eat too much.

Tonight she settled for the warm rotting of a dung heap, where she dreamed of nothing, for she hoped for nothing and expected nothing. It was as cold and dark inside her as out in the frosty night.

Morning brought rain to ease the cold, and the

kick of a boot in Brat's belly. Hunger. Brat hated the hunger most. Or was it the cold? She knew only that hunger and cold cursed her life and kept her waking and walking and working for no other reason than to stop the pain.

"Dung beetle! Dung beetle! Smelly old dung beetle sleeping in the dung."

Boys. In every village there were boys, teasing, taunting, pinching, kicking. Always they were the scrawniest or the ugliest or the dirtiest or the stupidest boys, picked on by everyone else, with no one left uglier or stupider than they but her. And so they taunted and tormented her. In every village. Always. She closed her eyes.

"Hey, boys, have off. You're mucking up the path and my new Spanish leather shoes. Away!

"And you, girl. Are you alive or dead?"

Brat opened one eye. A woman was there, a woman neither old nor young but in between. Neither fat nor thin but in between. An important-looking woman, with a sharp nose and a sharp glance and a wimple starched into sharp pleats.

"Good," said the woman. "You're not dead. No need to call the bailiff to cart you off. Now out of that heap and away."

3

The fierce pain in her stomach made Brat bold. "Please, may I have some'ut to eat first?"

"No beggars in this village. Away."

"Please, mistress, a little to eat?"

"Those who don't work don't eat."

Brat opened her other eye to show her eagerness and energy. "I will work, mistress. I am stronger and smarter than I seem."

"Smart enough to use the heat from the dung heap, I see. What can you do?"

"Anything, mistress. And I don't eat much."

The woman's sharp nose smelled hunger, which she could use to her own greedy purpose. "Get up, then, girl. You do put me in mind of a dung beetle burrowing in that heap. Get up, Beetle, and I may yet find something for you to do."

So Brat, newly christened Beetle, got up, and the sharp lady found some work for her to do and rewarded her with dry bread and half a mug of sour ale, which tasted so sweet to the girl that she slept in the dung heap another night, hoping for more work and more bread on the morrow. And there was more work, sweeping the lady's dirt floor and washing her linen in the stream and carrying her bundles to those cottages where a new baby was expected, for the sharp lady was a midwife. Beetle soon acquired a new name, the midwife's apprentice, and a place to sleep that smelled much better than the dung heap, though it was much less warm.

# 2.
# The Cat

BEETLE LIKED TO WATCH the cat stretching in the sunshine, combing his belly with his tongue, chewing the burrs and stubble out from between his toes. She never dared get close, for she was afraid, but even from a distance could tell that there was a gleaming patch of white in the dusty orange of his fur, right below his chin; that one ear had a great bite taken out of it; and that his whiskers were cockeyed, going up on one side and down on the other, giving him a frisky, cheerful look.

Sometimes she left bits of her bread or cheese near the fence post by the river where she first saw him, but not very often, for the midwife was generous only with the work she gave Beetle and stingy with rewards, and the girl was never overfed.

Once she found a nest of baby mice who had frozen in the cold, and she left them by the fence post for the cat. But her heart ached when she thought of the tiny hairless bodies in those strong jaws, so she buried them deep in the dung heap and left the cat to do his own hunting.

The taunting, pinching village boys bedeviled the cat as they did her, but he, quicker and smarter than they, always escaped. She did not, and suffered their pinching and poking and spitting in silence, lest her resistance inspire them to greater torments. Mostly she avoided them and everyone else, hiding when she could, scurrying along hidden, secret paths around the village, her head down and shoulders hunched.

One sunny morning, with stolen bread in her pocket for dinner and a bit of old cheese to share with the cat, Beetle started for the fence post. The boys were already there, holding the cat aloft by his tail. His hissing and screeching sounded like demons to Beetle, and she covered her ears.

"Into the sack with him, Jack," cried one boy. "We will see whether a cat can best an eel."

And the sack with eel and cat was tossed into the pond.

Beetle stayed hidden, more afraid to attract the taunts and torments of the boys than to lose the cat.

After a time the tumbling sack sank into the reedy water, and all was still.

"Ah, Jack, you was right. The eel took that cat right down." And the boy with the runny nose gave two apples to the boy with the broken teeth and they all went back to the fields.

Beetle waited a long time before she came out of hiding and waded into the muddy pond. With a stick broken from a nearby willow she searched through the reedy water, poking around and around the spot where the bag had gone down, working in bigger and bigger circles. Finally, near the edge of the pond, half out of the water, she found the bag, now soggy and still.

She dragged it out of the water, sat back on her heels, and watched. No movement. She poked it with her stick. Nothing.

"Cat," she asked, "are you drownt? I'd open the sack and let you out, but I be sore afraid of the eel. Cat?"

She kicked the bag with her dirty bare foot. Nothing. She left the bag and started back to the village. Came back. Left again. Came back again.

"The devil take you, cat," she cried. "I be sore afraid to open that sack, but I can't just let you be."

Taking a sharp stone, she slit the bag and ran behind a tree. Looking like the Devil himself, a shiny brown eel slithered out and made for the pond. And the bag was still again.

Beetle watched it. Nothing. She crept closer. Nothing. A sudden movement sent her scurrying back to the tree. And then nothing again. She crept up to the bag and found the scrawny, scruffy orange cat tangled in the soggy sack. Carefully she untangled his limp body and lifted him out of the bag by his front legs. "By cock and pie, cat, I would have you live."

Ripping a piece from the rag she called her skirt, she wrapped him tightly and ran her secret hidden route back to the village. She scooped a hole in the dung heap and laid the cat in it.

If Beetle had known any prayers, she might have prayed for the cat. If she had known about soft sweet songs, she might have sung to him. If she had known of gentle words and cooing, she would have spoken gently to him. But all she knew was cursing: "Damn you, cat, breathe and live, you flea-bitten sod, or I'll kill you myself."

All day the cat lay still in his cave in the dung heap. Beetle stole time from her chores and came often to see him, wrap her skirt more tightly around him, and make sure he still breathed. Twice she left little bits of cheese, but they were not eaten.

When she checked again after supper, as the sun was setting and the mist rising, he was gone and the cheese with him. Nothing in the cave in the dung heap but her bit of raggedy dress and a few threads from the sack, which he must have carefully combed from his fur before setting forth into the night.

And two days later (a holiday for the village, it being Lady Day, but not for Beetle, for the midwife would not feed those who did not work, even on Lady Day) there was the cat sitting on the fence post, licking his white patch to make it whiter still, waiting for Beetle and a bit of cheese. Finally Beetle came and they sat and ate their cheese together, to celebrate Lady Day. And Beetle told him what she could remember of her life before they found each other, and they fell asleep in the sun.

# 3.
# The Midwife

HER NAME WAS JANE. She was known in the village as Jane the Midwife. Because of her sharp nose and sharp glance, Beetle always thought of her as Jane Sharp. Jane Sharp became a midwife because she had given birth to six children (although none of them lived), went Sundays to Mass, and had strong hands and clean fingernails. She did her job with energy and some skill, but without care, compassion, or joy. She was the only midwife in the village. Taking Beetle gave her cheap labor and an apprentice too stupid and scared to be any competition. This suited the midwife.

Beetle slept on the cottage floor and ate two meals a day of onions, turnips, dried apples, cheese, bread, and occasional bits of bacon. This suited Beetle.

And so Beetle remained the midwife's apprentice as spring drew near and new green shoots appeared on the bare branches of shrubs and trees, and the villagers began ploughing the muddy fields for the summer crops. Beetle sometimes feared Jane Sharp was a witch, for she mumbled to herself and once a pail of milk curdled as she passed, but mostly she knew Jane was just what she first appeared, a woman neither young nor old, neither fat nor thin, with a sharp nose and a sharp glance and a wimple starched into sharp pleats.

Each morning Beetle started the fire, blowing on the night's embers to encourage them to light the new day's scraps. She swept the cottage's dirt floor, sprinkled it with water, and stamped it to keep it hard packed. She roasted the bacon and washed up the mugs and knives and sprinkled fleabane about to keep the fleas down. She dusted the shelves packed with jugs and flasks and leather bottles of dragon dung and mouse ears, frog liver and ashes of toad, snail jelly, borage leaves, nettle juice, and the powdered bark of the black alder tree.

In the afternoon Beetle left the village for the woods, where she gathered honey, trapped birds, and collected herbs, leeches, and spiders' webs. And the cat went with her.

When they were called, she accompanied the midwife to any cottage where a woman labored to birth her baby, provided that woman could pay a silver penny or a length of newly woven cloth or the best layer in the hen house. Beetle carried the basket with the clean linen, ragwort and columbine seeds to speed the birth, cobwebs for stanching blood, bryony and woolly nightshade to cleanse and comfort the mother, goat's beard to bring forth her milk and sage tea for too much, jasper stone as a charm against misfortune, and mistletoe and elder leaves against witches.

Beetle waited outside while the midwife did her magic within. The first time they were called to a cottage, Beetle tried to go in, but Jane slapped her, calling her clodpole and shallow-brained whiffler, and made her stay outside where she wouldn't get in the way.

Often she called Beetle in when it was over to clean out the soiled straw bed and wash the linen while Jane Sharp and the new mother sipped fever-few and nutmeg brewed in hot ale, and once she sent the girl back to the cottage to brew some black currant syrup to fight a new mother's fever. Beetle began to think perhaps she was kept out not because she was stupid, but to keep her in ignorance of the midwife's skills and spells. And she was right.

As the weather warmed and the villagers began digging long furrows in the field to take the seed, Beetle found herself doing more and more of the collecting and stewing and brewing, while Jane Sharp spent her time haggling over her fees. Twice the midwife refused to come to laboring mothers who had nothing to pay, and so the unfortunate women had to bring forth their babies with none but a neighbor to help.

The midwife's greed angered the villagers, but they needed her and so took out their anger not on Jane Sharp but on her apprentice, needed by no one. Beetle endured their anger and their taunts in silence and complained only to the cat, who listened and sometimes rubbed his head on her legs in sympathy.

When spring arrived with soft breezes and meadows grown green, the villagers began sowing early peas and barley, followed by the village boys who threw stones at the hungry birds trying to eat the seed. Jack and Wat threw stones too at Beetle and the cat who followed her, which made the villagers laugh. Beetle was only the midwife's stupid apprentice and no care to them.

One morning not too long before Mayday, Kate the weaver's daughter lay down in the field and declared her baby was coming right there and right then. Her father, Robert Weaver, and her husband, Thomas the Stutterer, tried to carry her back to their cottage, but she screamed and threw her arms about, so there was nothing to do but mound up some clean straw for a bed and bring the midwife out to the field.

Jane Sharp looked at the girl, settled the fee with Thomas, and rolled up her sleeves. She sent Beetle back to the cottage to pack a basket of necessaries. "And don't drop or forget anything, you with the brains of a chicken. And don't dawdle."

Beetle grabbed bottles off the shelf and bunches of dried herbs from the ceiling beams, surprised at how much she knew, how she could recognize the syrups and powders and ointments and herbs from their look and their smell, since the midwife could not write to make labels and Beetle would not have been able to read them even if she could.

Kate was laboring in the field, not at ploughing or sowing or weeding but at making a way for her baby into the world. As Beetle watched, Jane moved Kate up onto her knees and shouted, "Push, you cow. If an animal can do it, you can do it." And Kate pushed, as Jane the Midwife eased the child out of his mother and into her hands. It put Beetle in mind of the time she got the cat out of the bag. And she temporarily forgave the midwife her sharpness for the magic of her spells and the miracle of her skills.

After that Beetle took to watching through the windows when the midwife was called. In that way she learned that midwifery was as much about hard work and good sense and comfrey tonic as spells and magic.

# 4.
# The Miller's Wife

SUDDENLY IT WAS SUMMER and leaves erupted on every tree and bush in the village, and you could see flowers blooming by the road, in the churchyard, and in the hair of the young girls as they swung down the path to the village square. And just as the world burst into flowers, the midwife's cottage burst forth into bread—soft wheat bread for dinner and crunchy brown oat bread for supper and crusty rolls to dip into cool ale on a warm summer morning. Even Beetle shared in the sudden blooming of bread and didn't care to ask why until, her stomach finally full, she found her mind empty and casting about for something to figure out. She hit upon the mystery of the sudden abundance of bread. Where from? And how? And why?

And as she thought and watched and listened, Beetle noted that the midwife had taken to mysterious errands.

"Beetle, I must to the miller to have my oats ground to flour. Crush the bitter milkwort and boil the wormwood syrup while I am gone." And off the midwife would go. Without the oats.

Or, "Beetle, I am taking the comfrey tonic to Joan At-the-Bridge. See you finish boiling the goose grease for ointments." And off the midwife would go. With no comfrey tonic.

Or, "Beetle, I am going to feed the hens. Strain the nettle tea and pour it into clean flasks." And off the midwife would go, although Beetle knew the last hen had made soup weeks before and the hen house lay empty except for an occasional hopeful hungry dog.

Curious about this unusual behavior, Beetle began to follow the midwife when she went on these errands, creeping behind trees and under fences, careful to keep out of sight, and the cat stalked along behind her, so they looked like a Corpus Christi Day procession on its way to the churchyard—the midwife, the girl, and the cat. Each time, the midwife made for a field near the

Old North Road, and each time, Beetle feared to creep closer lest she be caught, so she could not discover what was happening in the field and whether it had anything to do with the bread.

One bright morning three days before Saint John's Eve, Beetle said, "Mistress, Meg from the manor dairy has asked for some of your goose grease ointment, for her legs ache from child carrying and she says nothing soothes like your goose grease ointment. She will pay you four eggs and a tot of butter."

The midwife, pleased both to be praised and to be paid, sent Beetle on her way, without telling her to return straightaway or setting chores for her to do after.

Beetle raced to the dairy, thrust the greasy ointment at Meg, grabbed the eggs and the butter, tied them in her skirt, and ran by her secret hidden way to the field by the Old North Road. She put the butter and eggs carefully in a hollow log and climbed a tree from which she could see the whole of the field. In no time there came Jane Sharp from the village and, from the other path, with a basket of bread steaming and warm, came the baker. Jane Sharp and the baker fell to such furious hugging and kissing, and him with a wife and thirteen children in their cottage behind the ovens, that the startled Beetle fell right out of that tree.

The baker caught her by her hair, and the midwife began shouting about how apprentices with nothing to do but spy needed a beating and more work. Then Jane hissed, "And don't you be telling anyone, Beetle, or I'll turn you out in the cold again and break both your knees before I do."

"And who would I be telling, then?" Beetle responded. "I don't talk to no one but the cat. And he don't care who you are kissin'."

With that, which had taken all her courage, Beetle gathered up the butter and the eggs, only one of which had broken, and marched away. The cat marching behind her heard Beetle mumbling, "You do not want to hear of this, for it is not mysterious at all, and was not an adventure, and there are no butterflies in it, or rats or mice or cream or moths, which is all you really care about."

Beetle muttered to the cat all the way back to the cottage, where she sat in the yard throwing green apples at the cow and waited for the midwife to return and give her a beating and more work.

When the sun was high in the sky, there came the miller running into the yard.

"We need the midwife!"

"She is not here."

"Where is she?"

"I cannot say." And Beetle could not, for she had promised she would not.

The miller grabbed Beetle's arm—"Then you, Dung Beetle, will have to do"—and off he dragged her by the arm to his cottage.

"I cannot," she said. "I am afraid. I do not know what to do. I cannot."

But he continued grabbing and dragging and soon Beetle was inside the miller's cottage. At any other time she would have enjoyed the visit, for never had she been in such a luxurious dwelling, with two rooms downstairs and a loft above and a high soft bed all enclosed by curtains such as the king or the pope must sleep in.

But this was now and not any other time, and on the high soft bed lay a large, pale woman, waiting for the midwife and getting Beetle instead. The miller thrust Beetle toward the bed. "The midwife's apprentice is here to help you, my dear. Things will go easier now." And he was gone.

The miller's wife lay uneasy in her great bed. She grabbed Beetle's arm and cried, "I no longer want this child. It was a mistake. Make it stop. I will do this no longer."

"I cannot," said Beetle. "I am sore afraid."

At that the miller's wife's cries increased in frequency and volume. Beetle tried to think what the midwife had said at moments like this. "Two eggs and a laying hen" and "Push, you cow" were the words that occurred to her, but when Beetle spoke them they did not have the same effect as when the midwife did.

"By the bones of Saint Cuthbert, they have sent me a nitwit! You lackwit! No brain! You think to touch me!" Screeching still, the miller's wife let go of Beetle's arm and began to throw at the girl whatever she could reach from her bed—a jug of warm ale, half a loaf of bread, a sausage, the brimming chamber pot. The terrified Beetle huddled in the corner as the woman rose from her bed to find more weaponry. Side of bacon. Bowl of stew. Walking stick. Soft felt hat and someone's breeches.

Half the village, it seemed, then pushed into the chamber to see the cause of the turmoil. The summer sun, the press of the curious crowd, and the exertions of the reluctant mother-to-be warmed the room to the point that Beetle felt she was in Hell, being attacked by demons, and her screams joined the rest.

Suddenly the door flew open and there stood the midwife, steam rising from her skin in the heat of the room. A pea-and-onion pudding landed at her feet. She was not smiling. "Out," she shouted. "Out!" she screamed. "*Out!*" she bellowed, and the room fell empty.

The midwife grabbed the miller's screeching wife and slapped her—once, twice, three and four times. Beetle lost count. Finally both the screaming and the slapping stopped. The midwife led the miller's wife back to the high soft bed and, holding her bruised face in her hands, poured a mug of wormwood tea down her throat.

When all was quiet, the miller's wife began her labors again, and finally, as Beetle told the cat later, "There come a baby."

It was then the midwife spied Beetle in her corner. "Idiot," she shouted. "Clodpole!" she screamed. "*Nincompoop!*" she bellowed. And she dragged Beetle out of the room, across the yard, and back to her cottage, by the very arm the miller had used to drag her away.

Beetle did not mind so very much. She was just grateful to be out of that room.

For weeks after, the midwife called her not Beetle but Brainless Brat and Clodpole and Good-for-Nothing, and Beetle worked twice as hard and talked only half as much, for she feared being turned cold and hungry out of the midwife's cottage.

## 5.
# The Merchant

Now it was high summer, with the hay drying in the fields and all the village praying for the rain to hold off until the grain was safely cut and stored away for winter.

The midwife, needing to replenish her stores of leather flasks, nutmeg, pepper, and the water in which a murderer had washed his hands, made plans to attend the Saint Swithin's Day Fair at Gobnet-Under-Green. Beetle had been to fairs, but only to beg a turnip or some pig bones for a stew, and never had her belly been full enough for her to lift her head and look around. She dearly longed to accompany the midwife, but still being Brainless Brat, she was afraid to ask. And so, the day before the midwife's departure, Jane set Beetle a score of tasks to accomplish in her absence and made ready to leave without the girl.

Beetle knew this was an important journey, for the midwife soaked herself in the millpond, dried her hair in the sun, and sharpened the pleats in her best wimple.

She sang to herself as she worked, a tuneless tune that Beetle supposed a witch's spell until she recognized it as "Summer Is A-coming In" sung by someone who lacked the practice and the heart and the sweetness to sing.

On her way back to the cottage, laden with newly washed clothes to spread in the sun, the midwife tripped over Walter the Blacksmith's second-best pig and fell, left leg twisted beneath her. Her furious oaths made Beetle truly fear she was a witch, for only someone who had truck with the devil could know such words.

Although bellowing that Beetle was stupid as a woodchuck and clumsy as a donkey in a dress, the midwife allowed the girl to help her into the cottage and onto her straw bed.

"Broken, by God's whiskers. Broken," she moaned, feeling her ankle, and she set about telling Beetle how to pack the boneset herbs and wrap the rags about the limb. Beetle feared this meant that because the midwife could not walk, she could not work, and thus would need Beetle's help no longer. Actually it meant that Beetle was to go to the Saint Swithin's Day Fair in the midwife's place. The joy in Beetle's heart warmed her insides and lit her face, even through the midwife's ranting about lack of wit and the dire consequences if she were to lose the silver pennies or spend too much or come home with the wrong things.

The blazing sun of Saint Swithin's morning dried the hay, gladdened the villagers, and saw Beetle on her way to Gobnet-Under-Green with four silver pennies, an onion and a hunk of bread, and a cheerful heart.

To get to Gobnet-Under-Green, Beetle took the road north that followed the river, passed the mill, turned east at Steven the Fletcher's cottage, cut across the abbey fields ablaze with the violet-blue flowers of the flax, turned north again at Barry-on-the-Birkenhead, then meandered easterly and northerly until it ended in the glory that was the Saint Swithin's Day Fair in the market square of Gobnet-Under-Green.

Beetle was too excited to eat along the way, so

she gave her bread and onion to a hungry goat that then followed her near all the way to Gobnet. When she arrived at the fair, she did not know whether her lightheadedness was from hunger in the sun or the thrill of being in the midst of such gaiety and color, and she did not care.

She passed through the forest of bright booths with flags and pennants flying, offering for sale every manner of wondrous thing—copper kettles, rubies and pearls, ivory tusks from mysterious animals, cinnamon and ginger from faraway lands, tin from Cornwall, and bright-green woollen cloth from Lincoln. She laughed at the puppets, wondered at the soothsayers, applauded the singers, and cheered for the racing horses. Her nostrils quivered at the smells of roasting meats and fresh hot bread and pies stuffed with pork and raisins, but her guts still trembled with excitement, and she was content just to smell.

As forenoon gave way to midday, Beetle wandered the fairgrounds. As midday turned to late afternoon, she remembered why she was there. She sniffed all the spices for free before buying nutmeg and pepper. The hangman was doing a brisk trade in murderer's wash water, but Beetle was at last able to secure a bottle. At the end of the Street of the Cup Makers, Beetle was told, just before the Church of Saints Dingad and Vigor, she could find the best prices on leather flasks. And so she did.

The merchant's booth was also filled with sundry other wares for wondering at: shiny brass needles, ribbons of red and lavender, copper spoons and bronze knives, boots of fine red leather with embroidery on the toes, and combs of polished wood and ivory. Beetle had never used more than her fingers to comb the burrs and thistles from her hair and probably could have lived her life so doing, but on one of the combs, between the two rows of teeth, was carved a sleeping cat. He looked so much like the cat Beetle knew that she ached to own it.

For long minutes she held the comb, looked at it this way and that, smelled the fragrant wood, and admired the sleeping cat. Then with a great sigh she put it down and turned to bargain with the merchant for the flasks. Although, or perhaps because, she was new at the bargaining game, Beetle handled it with such charming solemnity that the merchant took a fancy to the skinny young thing and, with a broad wink, threw the comb with the cat into the pack with the flasks. "Comb those long curls till they shine, girl, and sure you'll have a lover before nightfall." Another wink and the merchant turned to his next customer.

The comb was hers. Beetle stood breathless for fear someone would snatch it back. Never had she owned anything except for her raggedy clothes and occasional turnips, and now the comb with the cat was hers. The wink and the comment about her curls, though Beetle didn't know it, were also gifts from the generous merchant, and they nestled into Beetle's heart and stayed there.

Beetle settled the pack on her back and started for the village. In front of the Church of Saints Dingad and Vigor, she stopped to pull the comb through her hair. Curls. Were these tangles then curls? Beetle leaned over the horse trough and examined her hair in the still water. Definitely curls. Surrounding a thin little face with big eyes and a pointed chin. Big nose and big ears and the curliest hair at the fair. "This is me then, Beetle," she said. And looked again.

"Alyce, hey Alyce, I need you," said a man, pulling at Beetle's sleeve. She looked about for this Alyce.

"Alyce, here, what do this say?" he asked, thrusting a piece of leather with marks on it under Beetle's eyes.

She blinked and looked at him. "Who is Alyce?"

"Don't be funny, Alyce. These here marks are supposed to show my winnings on the horse race, and I need you to read them to be sure Cob the Groom is not cheating me. What do it say?"

"I'm not Alyce."

"Course you are." The man leaned over and peered closely into Beetle's face. "Wait," he shouted, spraying her with spit, "you're not Alyce! You look like Alyce. Where is Alyce? Alyce!" And off he went to find Alyce to make sure Cob the Groom was not cheating him on the horse race.

Beetle stood perfectly still. What a day. She had been winked at, complimented, given a gift, and now mistaken for the mysterious Alyce who could read. Did she then look like someone who could read? She leaned over and watched her face in the water again. "This face," she said, "could belong to someone who can read. And has curls. And could have a lover before nightfall. And this is me, Beetle." She stopped. Beetle was no name for a person, no name for someone who looked like she could read.

Frowning, she thought a minute, and then her face shone as though a torch were fired inside her. "Alyce," she breathed. Alyce sounded clean and friendly and smart. You could love someone named Alyce. She looked back at the face in the water. "This then is me, Alyce." It was right.

So the newly called Alyce shifted the pack on her shoulders, and with her head back and bare feet solid on the ground, she headed back to the midwife's cottage and never noticed when it grew cool and dark, for the heat and light within her.

# 6.
# The Naming

THE MIDWIFE HAD LOST ANOTHER TOOTH, and was hobbling about on her broken ankle, throwing copper pots and cooking spoons about the cottage in her anger at age and teeth and life. "Get out of my sight, Dung Beetle, before I squash you."

"Alyce."

"What did you call me?"

"Not you, me. Alyce. My name is Alyce."

"Alyce!" The midwife snorted like Walter Smith's great black horse, Toby. "Alyce! You look more like a Toad or a Weasel or a Mudhen than an Alyce." And as she punctuated each name with another pot thrown in the girl's direction, Beetle thought to go out.

Out was no punishment. Out was where there

were no kettles to stir, no bottles to fill, no smoky cooking fire. Out was where the air was cool, this summer morning, although the sun was warm. Out was where Beetle had spent most of her life.

Out was where the cat was. She wanted to tell him about her new name. Alyce. She had not dared yet say it aloud, but now that she had said it to the midwife, she wanted to tell everyone. "Alyce," she said to the cat, who rubbed and purred against her ankle. "I have a name now, cat, and you must also, so I can call you to breakfast on cold, foggy mornings. I will say some names, and you tell me when I have found the right one."

Beetle sat on the dusty ground, legs crossed. The cat sat and stared at her. "Willow?" she asked. "Purslane? Gypsy Moth? Lentil?" The cat just stared.

Beetle stood and walked toward the river, one hand across her belly, the other stuck in her mouth. Beetle was thinking. "Bryony? Millstone? Fleecy?"

"Gone completely daft, have you, Beetle?" said the miller as he passed.

"Alyce," said Beetle.

"Alyce who? Who Alyce?"

"I am Alyce," Beetle said. "Not Brat or Dung Beetle or Beetle. Alyce."

"Bah," said the miller. "May as well call a rock Alyce. Or a sheep. Alyce. Bah."

"Earth Pine?" continued Beetle to the cat. "Dartmoor? Cheesemaker? Holly? Pork?"

"Who you callin' Pork, you whiffle-brained dung beetle?" This from the blacksmith's lardy daughter, Grommet.

"The cat," Beetle said, "and I am Alyce."

"You are nitwit," Grommet Smith replied, and laughed as she waddled away.

Beetle sighed. This business of having a name was harder than it seemed. A name was of little use if no one would call you by it.

The cat wound himself around Beetle's ankle and purred. "Columbine? Cuttlefish?"

"Purr," the cat responded.

"Clotweed? Shrovetide? Wimble?"

"Purr," the cat responded.

"Horsera—"

"Purr," the cat demanded.

"Purr?" Beetle asked.

"Purr," the cat responded. And that was that.

While Beetle and Purr walked in the sunshine, waiting for the midwife's temper to cool enough for them to beg bread and cheese and an onion or two, the villagers brought in the last sheaves from the field and, hay harvest over, sat down to eat and drink and give thanks the rain had held off. Several of the village boys, with too much ale and too few wits, left the celebration looking for trouble to cause. And they found Beetle.

"Dung Beetle, give me a kiss," called the boy with red hair.

"Alyce," whispered Beetle, surrounded by boys and abandoned by the cat.

"She calls you Alyce, Will. Thinks you're a girl or a fine lady down from the manor. You friends with the dung beetle, Lady Alyce?" The boy with the broken teeth took another pull from his mug of ale and spat at Will.

Beetle took advantage of Will's distraction to duck beneath his arm, loop her skirts between her legs, and take off down the road to the river. The boys were faster, but they were drunk, and Beetle reached the river before they did. She looked for safety. An open field lay to her right. They could catch her there; they were not that drunk. Straight ahead was the river, but she could not swim. No one could. Water was for horses to drink and an occasional quick bath before weddings and such.

A sudden breeze rustled the leaves of a willow, as if it were calling to Beetle. Up she climbed into the branches, treed like a fox, waiting for what would happen next.

Pushing and shoving each other, the boys encircled the tree. "Dung beetle, dung beetle, you must be afeared, so far from your dung," they chanted. "Come down and we will take you home and lay you softly into the dung heap, deep, deep, deep into the dung heap."

More ale swigging and chanting and pushing and shoving. Suddenly the boy with red hair lost his footing on the slippery bank and tumbled into the churning river.

"Gorm, Will, get out of there," said snaggletoothed Jack.

"Can't," said Will, spitting water and floundering. "Throw me somethin' to grab."

But the water pulled Will under for a moment and the boys, grown sober and scared, knocked one another aside in their attempts to get out of there to a place they could claim they had never left when poor Will's drowned body was found. So that, when Will surfaced again, still spitting and floundering, no one was there but Beetle in the tree, looking down at him with her eyes great in her white face.

"Beetle, help me. Throw me somethin'."

Beetle shook her head. "I be too scared."

He disappeared again, and Beetle crept carefully out on an overhanging branch to see where he had gone. Sputtering, up he came, too full of water to call her name or beg for help, only looking at her as his arms slapped the water around him.

Beetle crept farther out on her branch. It dipped toward the river. Very slowly, inch by inch, as the boy struggled not to sink, she crept out until the tip of the branch nearly touched the water.

"Grab it, Will," she said. And he grabbed it. Slowly, slowly he pulled himself along the branch until, from his pulling and Beetle's weight, it cracked, and they both fell onto the riverbank.

Will lay there while Beetle watched to see was he alive or was he dead. Then he spat river water all over her skirt and she knew he lived to bedevil her again.

"You didn't run with the others," he said. "That were brave, Beetle."

"Naw, I be not brave," she said. "I near pissed myself. I did it for else you'd have drowned and gone to Hell, a drunken loudmouth bully like you, and I would have helped send you there and I could not have that, now, could I?"

"You have pluck, Beetle."

"Alyce."

"You have pluck, Alyce."

They looked at each other, pretended they hadn't, and went home. That night Beetle had a dream. The pope came to the village and called her Alyce and the king married the midwife and the cat laughed.

# 7.
# The Devil

IF THE WORLD WERE SWEET AND FAIR, Alyce (she must be called Alyce now) and Will would become friends and the village applaud her for her bravery and the midwife be more generous with her cheese and onions. Since this is not so, and the world is just as it is and no more, nothing changed. Most of the villagers still paid no attention to Alyce at all. Some were mean, like Grommet Smith, near as big as a dozen Alyces, who would sit on top of the girl so Jack and Wat could rub chicken manure into her hair, or the miller, who pinched her rump when she brought grain to the mill to be ground. And some were kind, or nearly so, like the baker's wife, who always asked Alyce how she fared on this fine day, and the redheaded Will, who threw fewer

40

stones at her since her saving of him and sometimes stopped the taunting altogether, saying, "Aw, this wag grows boresome. Dick's granny is hanging out the wash. Let's go tie knots in his breeches." And that is the way it was until the day the Devil walked about.

It started with the two-headed calf born to Roger Mustard's cow, Molly. And then a magpie landed on the miller's barn and would not be chased away. Suddenly the whole village saw witches and devils everywhere, and fear lived in every cottage.

Alyce, who had slept alone outside in the dark for most of her years, even at fearful times like All Hallows' Eve and Walpurgis Night, had never yet seen the Devil and had nothing to fear from the night. It was she, then, who was sent to fetch and carry and deliver messages after dark, while the villagers stayed in their smoky cottages. So it was that she saw much of what went on in the village and how people lived their lives and spent their time.

It was so quiet for a few days, with all the villagers inside and idle, that Alyce even had a little time to herself, to wander and think and plan, to watch and learn from old Gilbert Gray-Head about the carving and polishing of wood, and to ask questions of the priest about sin and evil and the Devil, humming to herself all the while.

Then, one damp autumn morning, Robert Weaver found strange footprints, which wound about the village and stopped suddenly at the door of the church. He called Thomas At-the-Bridge, who knew the ways of the woods and the tracks of the animals, to help him discover what sort of beast had been prowling about while they slept.

"Were it a weasel, Thomas?"

"No, that is a hoof. A weasel has toes."

"A goat, Thomas?"

"No, those prints are much too big for a goat."

"A pig?"

"No pig has dewclaws like that."

"A boar, Thomas?"

"With that delicate arch? Never a boar, Robert."

"What then, Thomas? What has hooves, is larger than a goat, and more delicate than a boar, and walks our village by night but stops outside the door of the church?"

By dinnertime all the village was talking of the strange animal that even Thomas At-the-Bridge could not identify. It only took a few incautious words and fearful whispers to convince them that the Devil had found their village and was looking for souls to lead into sin.

The next day, the strange delicate hoofprints were found walking around Dick's granny's cottage and through the barley field. Robert and Thomas and the priest, whispering paternosters, followed the prints all the way to the mill where, crossing themselves, they unlatched the door. The startled miller looked up, caught in the act of putting some of Dick's granny's grain into his own sacks.

"The Devil has indeed been here," cried the priest, "and he has tempted our miller into theft! But let us deal with this thief mercifully, for which of us could withstand the Devil?"

The villagers agreed, and so the miller who had listened to the Devil did not have his hands chopped off, but only stood one day in the rain with his millstone tied about his neck.

The next day all was quiet and it was hoped that the Devil had moved on to tempt another village, but as day passed into evening, Kate the weaver's daughter ran to the priest with her tale of seeing the Devil's prints leading to Walter Smith's barn. The priest and a brave band of villagers armed with rakes and pitchforks and sticks tied into crosses hurried to the barn. The priest sprinkled the door with holy water and threw it open. There, cuddled in the haymow, were Grommet, the smith's lardy daughter, and the pockmarked pig boy from the manor. The boy gathered his breeches and flung himself out the barn window. Grommet, being larger, moved more slowly and was caught.

For listening to the Devil, Grommet was made to spend the night in prayer and fasting. She wept, though for loss of pride or loss of supper none could say.

As the villagers sat down to their dinners the next day, Wat with the runny nose hurried down the road, calling, "I have seen him, a hairy demon with horns and claws and a great thrashing tail. He is on the road to the manor, looking for souls to take to Hell." Fully half the villagers ran away from the manor road, but the other half ran toward it, making sure the priest and the holy water preceded them.

There was no sign of the Devil on the manor road or in the woods on either side. Finally the villagers started home, and there near Roger Mustard's cottage were the Devil's prints, marching down the road, past Dick's granny's cottage, around Walter

Smith's barn, and up to the door of William the Reeve's cottage. Again the villagers flung open the door and again found the Devil had been at work, for there was Wat finishing off William Reeve's leg-of-mutton dinner.

The priest decided that Wat's gluttony and deceit were the fault of the Devil and not of the boy, so Wat's face was not branded, but William Reeve's bad-tempered pigs were in his care from that day on.

The next morning it was a larger group of villagers who followed the hoofprints to the woods where the broken-toothed Jack and his friends were clearing brush from Roger Mustard's field. Likely the Devil had tricked the boys into laziness, for they were found asleep and given a sound beating.

Two days went by with no sign of the Devil. The villagers grew calmer, thinking themselves fortunate not to have been tempted by the Devil and then found out in so public a fashion.

Then, on a misty morning, the Devil walked the village again. By this time no one expected to catch him, but they were eager to see whom they would find in what sin, so all the village followed the prints, except for the midwife, who was called to the manor at the last minute, and Alyce, who was elsewhere.

The parade of villagers laughed and gossiped out of the village and along the Old North Road. As they followed the prints through a field, they grew quiet. The prints stopped near a large tree and so did the villagers. From behind the tree came the call, "Is that you, Jane, my dove?" and out leaped the baker, holding a bunch of Michaelmas daisies and a basket of bread before him.

All was quiet. The baker's wife stepped forward and took the flowers as the villagers turned and walked away, leaving her to sort out what was the Devil's work and what the baker's.

After the departing villagers passed the river, at a spot where the water ran swift and deep, Alyce stepped out of the woods. She took something from under her skirt, threw it into the river, and followed the crowd home. And so it was that all (except the fortunate midwife) who had taunted or tormented Alyce were punished for their secret sins. After this, the Devil was never seen in the village again, and no one but Alyce knew why.

Several days later, in a village where the river meets the sea, there washed up on the banks two blocks of wood carved in the shape of the hooves of some unknown beast. No one could figure what they were or where they had come from, so eventually Annie Broadbeam threw them into her cooking fire and enjoyed a hot rabbit stew on a cool autumn night.

# 8.
# The Twins

THERE BEING FEW BABIES BORN that September, Alyce and the midwife spent their days making soap and brewing cider and wine. The first occupation stank up the air for miles around, what with goose grease and mutton fat boiling away in the kettle, so that Roger Mustard in the manor fields and the miller at his wheel near the river sniffed the air and said, "Someone be making soap today."

The second task would lay perfume on the air and gladden noses near and far. Alyce was greatly relieved when enough soap was made to wash all the linen in England, and brewing could begin.

First they cooked parsnips with sugar and spices and yeast and poured this into casks, where the fermenting mixture sang loud and sweet as it turned into wine. And the same they did with turnips.

Then Alyce, with baskets tied to each end of a pole, walked with the cat to the abbey gardens to gather fallen fruit. There, lying on the ground as if scattered by God just for Alyce, were apples, red and yellow, large and small, sweet and tart, firm and juicy. She tried a few, but unable to say whether she liked best the crisp, white-fleshed Cackagees, the small, sour Foxwhelps, or the mellow, sweet Rusticoats and Rubystripes, she tried a few more. The cat, not finding that apples were good to eat, batted the small ones across the yard, imagining they had ears and tails and other parts that made things worth chasing.

Returning to the village late in the day, with her baskets and belly full of apples, Alyce cut through the manor field, near where the villagers had dug a pit for the quarrying of gravel. From inside the pit came the cries of some fearsome thing—a beast or a witch or a demon—so she crossed herself and hurried her steps.

The demon was calling, "Come here to me, here to me." Alyce ran faster. Then stopped. The demon sounded mighty like Will, the boy with red hair who used to torment her and now did not so much.

"Are you demon or redheaded lout?" she called.

"Alyce, be that you?" came the response from the pit.

Cautiously she crept to the edge and looked over. It was redheaded lout, and with him his cow.

"Alyce, you must help me. Tansy has fallen into the pit and I cannot get her to climb out, for she is about to have her calf and will not move. Come and help me."

"I am no midwife for cows, Will Russet," she called.

"She needs your help, Alyce, and so do I."

"Indeed I am no midwife at all, Will Russet, and I do not know what to do."

"Come over and I will tell you. This is Tansy's first calf but not mine."

At that Tansy called out, low and mournful and full of pain and fright. Alyce could not bear to leave her like that, so she put down her baskets of apples and slid into the pit.

Will grinned at her. "Good for you, Alyce. Here, hold her head. Keep her quiet. Sing something soft."

"I do not know any singing, Will Russet."

"Croon a song without words, then. Just make sweet noises."

So Alyce did, although none would have called them sweet but she and the boy and the cow. And perhaps the cat, who lay above, where Alyce had left him, carefully licking the soft pink pads of his feet.

"Hold her, Alyce. Rub her head and belly. If we can but calm her, God will tell her and the calf what to do."

Alyce sang and rubbed, calling the cow Sweetheart and Good Old Girl as she heard Will do, and the boy pushed and pulled and worked as hard as the cow. Several times they near gave up, but Alyce always found one more song or one more rub inside her, and Will loved Tansy like she was his babe and not his cow, and so the tired pair kept on.

Finally, as day darkened into evening, there came the feet of a calf. Then more feet. And more. "Twins, Alyce!" cried Will. "You have brought me great luck, for Tansy be having twins!"

So she was, and soon two slippery, shiny, brand-new calves were lying in the dirt of the pit, and Tansy was licking and nuzzling them gently.

Once Alyce and Will took the calves upon their

shoulders and scrambled from the pit, so too did Tansy, not willing to stay alone in that hard, dark, and calfless place. Like a holy procession they returned to the village, the boy and the girl and the newborn twins and the cow and the cat.

Will, so happy with twice the bounty he expected from Tansy, made sure to tell everyone of his luck and of the great help Alyce had been to him, and Alyce felt her skin prickling with delight, although she got in a muck of trouble for being so long about apple gathering and then losing the baskets as well as the fruit, for in the excitement of the twin calves they were forgotten and left behind and never seen again.

As September turned to October and October to November, through all those days, Alyce grew in knowledge and skills. The midwife, busy with her own importance, did not notice. Alyce, grown accustomed to herself, did not notice. But the villagers noticed, and as October turned to November and the ghosts walked on All Hallows' Eve, they began to ask her *how* and *why* and *what can I.* Sometimes for her help or advice someone would pay her a ribbon or an egg or a loaf of cheese or bread, which she always gave to the midwife, as if

Alyce herself were just the midwife's hand or arm, doing the work and receiving the pay but taking no credit for the task.

One morning as they sat under the old oak tree eating their breakfast bread, Alyce told the cat again about the birth of Tansy's twins. "All shiny they were, and sticky to touch. I did not even know them, but I loved them so much." This sounded to her like a song, so she made singing sounds as she had that day in the gravel pit, and then sang her words to the tune:

> *All shiny they were,*
> *And sticky to touch.*
> *I did not even know them,*
> *But I loved them so much.*

And so it was that Alyce learned about singing and making songs. Her song brightened the cold gray day so that a cowbird thought it was spring and began to sing in the old oak tree.

# 9.
# The Bailiff's Wife's Baby

"A GOOD NUT YEAR means a good baby year," the midwife said as she sent Alyce and her nutting basket to the woods to see what kind of a year it would be. All day Alyce shook the young trees, climbed into the old ones, and gathered the hard-shelled bounty that fell. Hazelnuts, walnuts, chestnuts, almonds mounded in her basket and stirred her hunger with thoughts of hot roasted nuts on cold winter nights. That was the limit of her imaginings, for never had she heard of almond cream, pickled walnuts, or eels in chestnut sauce, such as they ate at the manor or the homes of rich merchants in London and York.

Coming back from the woods, she saw the boys teasing the cat. She took a handful of nuts, the biggest and hardest and heaviest in her basket, and heaved them at the boys.

"Touch that cat again," she shouted, "and I will unstop this bottle of rat's blood and viper's flesh and summon the Devil, who will change you into women, and henceforth each of you will giggle like a woman and wear dresses like a woman and give birth like a woman!"

She was too startled by her outburst to be afraid. The boys were too startled by her outburst to move. And so Purr the cat escaped and Alyce reached the midwife's cottage unharmed, and until they were quite old the boys in the dark of night sometimes were afraid that the midwife's bottle actually had the power to make them into women. It was fortunate that the boys never tested Alyce's magic, for the bottle she shook so fiercely at them was naught but blackberry cordial she was to deliver to Old Anna on her way home from nutting in the woods, and although it would have made the boys purple and sticky, no harm would have befallen them and never would they have been able to give birth like a woman.

That night Joan the bailiff's wife sent for the midwife. Alyce lighted Jane's way through the

gloomy night with a rushlight that hissed and sput-
tered in the mist. The midwife chased Joan's husband, her young son, two pigs, and a pigeon out
of the cottage, bade Alyce wait for her in the yard,
and slammed the cottage door.

Alyce dozed there in the wet through the long
hours of the night. Shortly after dawn, when the
sky turned not rosy and welcoming as it does in
summer but merely a lighter shade of gray, the
midwife kicked her awake. "Up, Beetle, and to the
cottage for cowslip, mugwort, and pepper. By the
Fourteen Holy Helpers, Joan will have to sneeze this
baby out!"

When Alyce returned, the midwife was waiting
in the yard, her bottles and herbs and linen neatly
packed in the basket beside her.

"Has Joan then sneezed her baby out already?"
Alyce asked.

"Ha!" responded the midwife. "This child looks
never to come out. You go in and wipe Joan's face
and I will be back as soon as I can. Lady Agnes at
the manor has started her labor and wishes me to
attend her. They will pay me in silver, and the
bailiff in chickens and beans. God and the babies
willing, I will have it all."

Alyce began to cry. "I do not know what to do, Mistress Jane. Do not leave me. Do not leave her. I do not know what to do."

Alyce was silenced with a sharp slap. "Do nothing, you lackwit fool," the midwife spat. "She will never deliver that baby. It will die unborn, and I will take it dead from her when I return. Let her labor while I see to the Lady Agnes. I will come back, do what must be done, and collect both fees."

Alyce snuffled into her sleeve, leaving her nose dirty and red and no drier than it was.

"Do nothing," repeated the midwife. "In her state, Joan will not even remember that I left. Do nothing and say nothing!" And off the midwife ran, up to the manor where warm fires blazed and the laboring mother was soothed with wine and syrups and kind words. Alyce turned back to the dark, cold, nearly empty cottage, took a deep breath, and went in.

She couldn't see the figure on the bed at first for all the smoke, and then realized that the writhing mound was Joan, the bailiff's proud wife who washed her linen each week and never let herself be seen without shoes even in summer, and there she was, a moaning, mewling mound on a straw bed.

Alyce covered her mouth and her eyes and turned to go. She could tell the midwife she had waited with Joan. Who was to know if she sat on the stoop until she heard the crinkle of the midwife's starched wimple?

"Let me die. By the bones of Saint Mildred, let me die. Or help me to die." The moaning, mewling mound spoke, not, as Alyce expected, frantically or madly, but calmly and reasonably, asking for death. To Alyce it sounded all the more frightening and strange, as if a goose had spoken, or an egg, or the dung heap in the yard.

"Beetle, is that you?" Joan asked. "Where is the midwife?"

"Out but to relieve herself, mistress. She will be back soon, and then your babe will be born."

"Don't sham me, Beetle. I know this babe is stuck and will never be born and we will both die soon and why not now? Surely the midwife has something in her basket to help us along?"

"Shh, mistress. 'Tis but pain and fright make you speak so, for else you'd never think of sending yourself to Hell and the baby with you."

"Hell indeed, Beetle, and no worse than this suffering." Suddenly the proud, reasonable Joan became again the moaning, mewling mound. Then, as the hot pains invaded her body, she shouted and thrashed and flailed, shrieking and kicking.

Alyce betook herself to the cottage door, ready to run from this horror. But the memory of the proud, frightened Joan of a moment ago kept her inside. And she asked herself, What would the midwife do were she here? What had Alyce seen her do from cottage windows all this year when the babe would not come and the mother looked to scream and thrash herself to death? What had Will done in that gravel pit to help Tansy with the calves who would not be born?

Alyce took another deep breath and returned to Joan's side. She gave her mugwort in warm ale to drink and spoke soothingly, calling her Sweetheart and Good Old Girl. She warmed oil over the fire and rubbed her head and belly, as she had the cow's. She did not know the spells or the magic, so gave Joan all she had of care and courtesy and hard work.

So it was that in the middle of the night, when the monks were rising from their beds for midnight prayers, and in the towns revelers were returning home full of beef and wine, and at the manor the midwife was delivering Lady Agnes of her first son, so it was that a calmer, more rested Joan, with the kind attention of the midwife's apprentice, brought forth a daughter, feet first but perfectly formed, whom she called Alyce Little.

Alyce had washed Alyce Little and wrapped her in clean linen and laid her in her father's arms before Jane the Midwife bustled up the path and into the cottage. Jane made some remarks, which no one believed, about having left for just an instant, and stuck her hand out for her fee.

The bailiff said, "We have no need of you, Jane. Your helper has taken care of us with her two strong hands and her good common sense."

At that, Alyce felt so much pride and satisfaction that she had to let them out somehow, and so she smiled, which felt so good that she thought she might do it again. Facing the midwife's jealous anger, she went back to their cottage, ate some cold soup and hard bread, lay down on her straw mat by the fire, and had a dream about her mother, which upon waking she could not remember.

# 10.
# The Boy

AFTER THIS, when the midwife was summoned to attend a mother, Alyce took to stealing her way inside the woman's cottage, hiding in the shadows so as not to be noticed, watching closely to see what the midwife did and how and why. She took and stored in her brain and her heart what she heard the midwife say and do about babies and birthing and easing pain.

She discovered that an eggshell full of the juice of leeks and mallows will make a labor quicker, that rubbing the mother's belly with the blood of a crane can make it easier, that birthwort roots and flowers can strengthen contractions in a reluctant mother, and that, if all else fails, the midwife can shout into the birth passage, "Infant, come forward!

Christ calls you to the light!" She found that mouse ear and willow can help stop bleeding and that a tea of anise and dill and bitter milkwort will help when milk will not come.

She learned that newborn infants are readily seized by fairies unless salt is put in their mouths and their cradles, that a baby born in the morning will never see ghosts, and that a son born after the death of his father will be able to cure fevers.

Alyce thought the midwife had more skills with herbs and syrups and spells than Will Russet, but Will delivered babies just as well and was much kinder to the mother. Alyce thought if she needed a midwife, she would rather someone like Will than Jane Sharp, for all her spells and syrups.

Early one cold November day, before the pale, watery sun could light up the morning sky, Alyce left the midwife's cottage and hurried to the cow-shed to see Tansy's twins, now called Baldred and Billfrith after the saintly local hermits, and give them some parsnip tops to munch. There, huddled as close to Tansy as her calves, lay a sleeping boy, blue in his lips, frost in his hair, and tears frozen on his thin dirty cheeks. Her coming startled him awake and he jumped to his feet.

"I be leaving, mistress," he said. "I took nothing. I hurt nothing. I be going."

Alyce grabbed his arm. "Wait, boy. I mean you no harm. Who are you?"

"I be nobody, mistress. I go."

"Everybody is somebody and so are you. Want some breakfast?"

From the sleeve of her gown Alyce pulled the parsnip tops meant for the cows and some cheese she had saved for the cat and fed instead the hungry boy.

She watched him as he ate. Six, he was. Maybe a little older, for all he was so small and thin. He looked a little like her, now she thought about it. A sudden pleasure inside her warmed her hands as she reached out to smooth the boy's hair.

"Next time you be much warmer nestled in the dung heap these cold days," she told him. "I know."

He finished the cheese and looked up at her. "Bread?"

"Bread. I'll go fetch some. You stay here."

Alyce ran for the cottage, found a bit of bread she had hidden away for the cat, ignored the midwife's questions and demands, and started back for the cowshed.

63

The boy was running down the road toward her, pursued by several much bigger boys shouting and threatening with their pitchforks and rakes.

"Beggar! Thief! Ragtag!" they shouted as the boy crashed right into Alyce and sent them both sprawling to the ground.

"Have off, Dick," said Alyce, "or I be telling your granny who drank that ale she hid for herself. And you, Jack Snaggletooth, I still have that bottle of rat's blood!"

As the boys backed away, Alyce stood, brushing the mud from her skirt with one hand and holding on to the boy with the other.

"Have off, I said," she repeated, moving toward them.

"Corpus bones, Beetle. We were but wagging him since you are no sport no more."

And the boys moved off to torment someone else until they were found, slapped, and sent to work.

When Alyce and the boy, who said his name was Runt, got back to the midwife's cottage, Jane was out seeing to Kate the weaver's daughter, who was having trouble with her milk. Alyce brought the boy into the yard, cleaned his face with her skirt, and combed the straw from his hair, all the while telling him that Runt might be a good name for a small pig but never for such a likely-looking boy as he, and that she would help him find a place to sleep and something regular to eat but he would have to have a real name, for she was not taking anywhere anyone named Runt.

"What is your name?" the boy asked.

"Alyce," said Alyce.

"Then I be Alyce, too."

"You cannot be Alyce, for it is a name for a girl."

"What then is the king's name?"

Alyce did not know, so she hid the boy in the chicken house and went about the village asking folks what was the king's name.

"Longshanks," said the baker.

"Hammer," said Thomas At-the-Bridge.

"The Devil Hisself," said Brian Tailor, who was a Scot and so had reason to feel that way.

"Just 'the king' is all," said several.

"Edward," said the bailiff. "The king's name is Edward."

"Edward," said Alyce to the boy.

"Then Edward is my name," said Edward, who used to be called Runt. Alyce nodded.

She could see the midwife coming in the distance, so Alyce spat on her fingers and rubbed a bit of stubborn dirt off Edward's cheek. "Go," she said, "up that road to the manor. They are hiring boys to help with the threshing. Tell them Jane the Midwife sent you and bid them remember the good job she did delivering Lady Agnes' stubborn son. Now go."

Edward shook his head and grabbed a piece of her skirt in his fist, but she put him off. So he straightened his tunic and went, looking back once to throw a brave, shaky grin at Alyce.

The returning midwife, angry at Alyce for ignoring her earlier, set her to do all the least pleasant chores: roasting frogs' livers, boiling snails into jelly, stripping the thorns from dogberry roses.

But Alyce minded little, for she thought not of her tasks but of Edward's face and the abundance of bread and cheese up at the manor looking for a hungry boy's belly to fill.

## 11.
# The Leaving

ALYCE WAS SITTING BY THE FIRE one cool November morning, tying up birch twigs for a broom, when a pounding came at the door. Jane opened the door to Matthew Blunt, whose mother was about to have another baby and wanted Alyce to come and help.

"By the bones of Saint Polycarp, who is Alyce?" bellowed the midwife.

The boy jerked his head towards Alyce. "Her. Yer apprentice. My mum said Alyce helped her sister Joan, the bailiff's wife, when no one else could, and so she will have no one but Alyce."

"Her? The dung beetle?" The midwife quivered in disbelief. "You are asking for her, who knows nothing and fears to try and does only what little I bid her and that none too well?" She cracked Alyce on the cheek.

"My mum will have no other," repeated the boy.

The midwife looked a bit like a mad dog as she spat and spluttered and tried to get words out past all the anger in her mouth. "Go then, 'Alyce.' Such treachery! Such thievery! Eating my bread and stealing my mothers! Go!"

When she began to throw cooking pots their way, Alyce and the boy lit out and ran all the way to Adam Blunt's cottage. Alyce stood outside for a minute, surprised at having been asked for and not knowing whether to be pleased, until the boy nudged and pushed her to the door. She wiped her hair from her eyes, licked her lips, and went in.

The cottage was warm and Emma Blunt even warmer, what with her efforts to have this baby and be done with it. Alyce rubbed and crooned and fussed, as she had with the bailiff's wife. She fed Emma on raspberry leaf tea and comfrey wine. She built up the fire, closed all the windows, and three times called the baby forth. Then she sent Matthew to search for birthwort root, put out the fire, and opened all the windows. But the baby would not come, as if he were holding tight to his mother, reluctant to be separate and alone, and Alyce, although able to ease a willing baby into the world, had no idea how to encourage a reluctant one.

So as the day passed from morning to midday and Emma tossed on her tumbled linen and still there was no sign of a baby, Alyce, doubtful and uncertain without the midwife or at least Will Russet to tell her what to do and unwilling to get herself or Emma into trouble, stood back from the bed and said, "I cannot do it."

She washed Emma's face, smoothed her wet hair, took a deep breath, and sent Matthew back to the cottage for the midwife.

Emma and the unborn baby rested from the morning's struggle, so all was quiet until the midwife roared in, like wind before rain, blasting everyone out of her way as she set about attending to mother and babe.

She insulted and encouraged, pushed and poked, brewed and stewed and remedied. Anointing her hands with cornmeal and oil, she rubbed and kneaded, pulled and tugged, and turned that baby from both the inside and the outside until finally he was in a position to come out. Then she slapped Emma's great bulge of a belly, lifted her from behind by her shoulders, and gave her a good shake.

All was chaos, noise and heat and blood, until finally over the tumult Alyce could hear the cries of a baby, the moans of a tired mother, and the laughter of the triumphant midwife.

Alyce backed out of the cottage, then turned and ran up the path to the road, she didn't know why or where. Behind her in that cottage was disappointment and failure. The midwife had used no magic. She had delivered that baby with work and skill, not magic spells, and Alyce should have been able to do it but could not. She had failed. Strange sensations tickled her throat, but she did not cry, for she did not know how, and a heavy weight sat in her chest, but she did not moan or wail, for she had never learned to give voice to what was inside her. She knew only to run away.

So it was that on a crisp, sunny Martinmas afternoon, while the villagers slaughtered their cattle and pigs for winter meat, while Meggy Miller stirred a sheep's blood pudding for supper, while Will Russet and Dick gathered beech and oak and ash and chestnut for winter fires, while Alnoth the Saxon cleaned the manor privies and cursed God for making him a peasant and not a lord, while the boy Edward ate a bowl of herring soup and thought of the warm corner of the manor kitchen that was to be his, while Emma, the bailiff's wife's sister, kissed her new son on his tiny red nose and fell asleep with him at her breast, while the life of the village went on, Alyce turned her back on all that she knew and that had come to be dear to her and headed up the road from the village to she knew not where. And the cat went with her.

## 12.
# The Inn

THE CAT WAS HUNGRY. He pushed at the lumpish weight that was holding him down, spitting and scratching until Alyce shifted and he could crawl out to see what creatures there were about that were both good to eat and easy to catch. His exertions woke Alyce and she sat up and looked about her.

At first she made to stretch and smile and face a fine new day; then she remembered. It was afternoon, she was a failure, and she had run away. It was beginning to rain and she faced a night outside alone in the wet. She curled up again into a wet soggy ball.

"I am nothing," she whispered to herself. "I have nothing, I can do nothing and learn nothing.

I belong no place. I am too stupid to be a midwife's apprentice and too tired to wander again. I should just lie here in the rain until I die." And she fell again into a dreamless sleep.

But the next morning her young body, now used to a roof and warm food on cold mornings, pricked and pained her until she awoke. It was still raining and she was still a homeless failure. She stood up, picked some of the leaves from her hair, wiped her drippy nose on her sleeve, and looked around.

She knew where she was. Behind her were the village, Emma, the midwife, and failure—she could not go back there. She could not stay here in the rain waiting to die, for she was too cold and hungry and uncomfortable and alive. So she went on ahead. The cat stalked behind, stomach empty and feet wet, but unwilling to let Alyce go on without him.

An hour's walk brought them to the crossroads where the road from the village met the road to the sea, and there Alyce could see, through the wet November dawn, a light.

It was an inn. Alyce had never been in such a place, where anyone could find a bed or dinner provided he had the coins. Alyce did not have the coins, but she had two strong hands and an empty belly to fill, and she was soon at work in the kitchen, trading her labor for bread and a bed out of the rain. Purr made himself useful keeping mice from the barley and tasting everyone's cheese.

The inn was really no more than a large stone cottage with a room over the big kitchen, a loft above the stable, and tables in the hall good for sleeping on or under. The innkeeper was called John Dark, for he was nearly sightless, but none so blind that he could not find an untended mug of ale anywhere on the table or pinch a plump cheek as it passed. Most work about the inn was done by his wife, the round and rosy Jennet, who could carve a fowl with one hand, turn cream into butter with the other, and still have one left over to hoist a noisy guest by his shirt front and chuck him out the door.

"Oskins, boskins, chickadee," Jennet said next day to Alyce. "You are such a help to me that I would you would stay on awhile." Alyce had nowhere to go, so she stayed, grateful that she had found work she was not too stupid to do, even if it was only scouring the tables with river sand or skinning an eel for a pie.

Alyce worked hard and lived mostly on beans, bread, and Jennet's bad beer. Each week the autumn grew colder and wetter, and the inn, although dirty and drafty, was much cozier than any barn or dung heap to be found outside, so she remained, empty of heart. She would not think about her months in the village or Will Russet or the bailiff's Joan or the midwife, for such thinking brought the tickling to her throat again, but sometimes the smell of garbage or of apples baking would make the village so alive in her mind that she would look up quickly, certain she had been magically taken back there again, and her eyes would blink in hope and dread. Sometimes too she thought of the boy she had sent to the manor and wondered how he fared and if she had at least done that right.

Soon it was Christmas and the inn teemed with folk going away or coming home. Alyce hung holly and ivy from the charred beams in the hall. Musicians with their rebecs and gitterns and sackbuts came to drink and stayed to play. Ducks and geese on great skewers were turned in the roaring fire until they were golden and juicy and so fragrant that the cat and the mice came in from the stables hoping for a bite or two. It was all colorful and warm, but Alyce enjoyed none of it. Her heart heavy, her eyes blank, and her mouth as tight as a hazelnut, she went about the business of Christmas as if she were mucking out a stable, muttering over and over to herself, "I am nothing, have nothing, belong nowhere."

January dawned frosty and gray and stayed that way, and Alyce stayed, too. Just before gray January turned into black February, she noted a thin, brown-coated back hunched over a table close to the fire and realized she had seen that same brown-coated back for weeks now, hunched in the same way over the same table before the same fire.

Alyce began to watch the man, not knowing he had long watched her and wondered what could so blight a person so young. He was long and skinny as a heron, with black eyes in a face that looked sad, kindly, hungry, and cold. She thought at first he had the pox, for his long face, long nose, and long yellow teeth were all spotted, but it proved to be only ink, splattered as he pushed his quill pen furiously along. Corpus bones, she thought. He is writing! That is a man who can write! She kept her eyes down as she served him his bread and ale, barely daring even to breathe the same air, she who was too stupid to be a midwife's apprentice.

While they watched the big sow drop seven piglets one dark afternoon, Jennet told Alyce about the brown-coated man. Magister Reese, it was said, was a renowned scholar. Staying at the inn for the winter, he was working off his room and board by keeping accounts and penning letters for guests while he finished writing what was rumored to be a great and holy book.

Alyce studied the man. She noted that John Dark liked to sit near him, for he was careless of his ale; that Jennet made sure to give him the smallest portion or the toughest meat, for he ate what he was given and never complained; that he never scolded Tam the kitchen boy, who had been kicked by a horse and was not right in the head, even when Tam spilled beer or bacon fat on his papers; and that only the geese seemed awed by him, scattering hurry-scurry when he entered the inn yard lest another tail feather go for a quill pen.

Alyce took to sweeping that corner of the floor more carefully and scrubbing that end of the table more frequently, hoping to see what he was writing and what it might look like, for her curiosity overcame at last even her bleak despair. After a while he tried to speak to her, but she would only clutch tighter to her broom and sweep furiously in silence, so instead he took to talking to the cat.

"This, puss," he said, shifting the sleeping animal off the page he was writing, "is my masterwork, an encyclopaedic compendium I call 'The Great Mirror of the Universe Wherein You Can Find Reflected All of the World's Knowledge, Collected by Myself, Magister Richard Reese, M.A., and Dedicated to His Ampleness the Bishop of Chester,' so called for he is ample in all the world's virtues." Or "See how I can make the ink blacker by mixing soot with the boiled oak galls." Or "This, cat, is a P, as in *puss* or *pork* or *plum pudding*." Or "The letter S must be made just so, never thick or wiggly or with an extra curve at the end, but just so."

The cat listened carefully, although sometimes he lost patience with the tutoring and began to bite at the tantalizingly moving pen. And Alyce, too, listened, so that she learned some letters as the cat learned. She liked best the O, the D, and the G, for they looked friendly. Z seemed mean, X wicked; and W always made her yawn. Q was by far the most beautiful, she thought, even if it could not stand alone and must be accompanied everywhere by the compliant U.

Sometimes at night, when the cat's belly was full and he had no need to prowl about looking for supper, he let Alyce cuddle him against her as they went to sleep and tell him more about what she had learned that day: how A began *Alyce* and *apple* and *ark*, when to put a tail on the S, and what letters might be made to spell *Purr*, even though he must, she thought, know these things as well as she. During the day, when not boiling or sweeping or chopping or skinning, she wrote letters in the frost on the woodpile with a twig, scraped them into the soot of the chimney wall with the handle of the broom, and stuck her finger in the mutton soup and wrote them on the table in the kitchen. At night she found them written out in stars in the clear cold sky.

Once Alyce knew all the letters and a number of combinations, Magister Reese began teaching the cat words, reading aloud bits of wisdom from his great encyclopaedia. As a result Alyce heard about the heavenly planets circling the earth in hollow transparent spheres, about the great empire of the Romans that once stretched all the way to Britain, about the faraway island of giant ants who walk upright and mine for gold. She learned about the four humors that govern the body, how to plant corn by moonlight, and where the Antipodes are. And still he had not said a word to her.

When one day he threw away a page he had ruined with an inkblot, Alyce snatched it up and stuffed the stiff vellum into her bodice. Each night before she blew out the last candle, she would labor over the page, picking out letters and sometimes even words that were familiar to her.

One showery afternoon when raindrops sparkled like fairy dew on the new green leaves, Magister Reese sat dreaming over his mug of Jennet's thin, bitter ale. Winter was nearly over and his book far from finished. What was he to do next? Should he stay or go? "What do I want to do?" he asked himself. Spying Alyce sweeping her way toward him, he asked her, "What do I want?" And then, pointedly, "And what, inn girl, do *you* want?"

Alyce stopped still. She thought just to sweep away, but the shock of his addressing her directly was lost in that intriguing question. What did she want? No one had ever asked her that and she took it most seriously. What do I, Alyce the inn girl, want?

She chewed on a lock of her hair to help her think. What did people want? Blackberry pie? New shoes? A snug cottage and a bit of land?

She thought all that wet afternoon and finally, as she served Magister Reese his cold-beef-and-bread supper, she cleared her throat a time or two and then softly answered: "I know what I want. A full belly, a contented heart, and a place in this world."

Magister Reese looked up at her in surprise. "You ask a lot for an inn girl. I thought you'd say a sweetheart or a yellow ribbon for your black hair."

"No, this is what I want, but it is my misfortune instead to be hungry, out of humor, and too stupid to be a midwife's apprentice."

"None so stupid," he said. "You can read as well as the cat."

Alyce smiled. And so winter turned to spring.

# 13.
# Visitors

JENNET WAS WELL CONTENT WITH ALYCE. The girl didn't steal food, sneak ale, or dally with the guests. She was strong, willing, undemanding; and she had enough common sense to do what she was bid and ask no questions. So Alyce laid fires and swept floors and carried water all that spring.

She was learning also to overyeast the bread and weight the mugs, so that much of what she served was merely air or iron. She stirred who-knows-what poor wild thing into the stew and called it beef or rabbit. When important-looking guests arrived and Jennet called to Alyce in a loud voice to put clean sheets on the big bed, Alyce knew she was to do no such thing, but the important-looking guests overheard and were comforted by the thought.

"Thundering toads," Jennet would say, "I am but a poor woman with this wretched inn and a blind man to care for. I am sure God does not begrudge me my little economies."

And she got by with it because she was so round and rosy and merry and, with it all, so fair, in that she cheated everyone the same.

As spring burst into May and the trees were all flowers and Magister Reese decided to stay for one more season, there came to the inn a comely young man who acted so lordly Alyce thought he must be a knight or a mayor but proved to be the carpenter's assistant from the manor. She watched and listened to him, and finally while serving his mutton pie was bold enough to ask, "The boy Edward, who arrived at the manor for the threshing. Do you know him? How does he fare?"

"Never heard of him."

"A little boy, near seven, although small and puny for his age."

"Never seen him. Mayhap he run off or died or got eaten by a goat." The carpenter's assistant grinned at this with mutton stuck between his lordly white teeth.

Alyce's heart thumped. Was she too stupid then

83

even to have helped Edward? Was he not safe at the manor as she thought but somewhere unknown and unsafe and unfit? Or did the lordly young man just not bother to notice small boys?

Then on a day so like summer that the apple trees were tricked into fruit, there came another visitor. Alyce had just finished watering the beer and was kneading sawdust into the pie crust when she heard the rumble of a cart on the inn path. A load of wood had come for the kitchen, and walking behind the wagon was the redheaded boy from the village, Will Russet.

Alyce forgot for a moment that she was no longer the midwife's apprentice but now a failure and, wiping her floury hands on her skirt, ran outside.

"Will! Will Russet! It's me, Alyce."

"Alyce," he called. "We was wondering where you had got to and were you all right. What be you doing here?"

The sunshine faded from Alyce's face. "Skinning rabbits and sweeping floors and mucking out the privy. I am the inn girl."

"And a prettier inn girl the world never saw," said Will, "or you would be if you ever got that flour and dirt off yer face. Come talk to me while I unload the cart."

Alyce spat on her fingers and rubbed her face, but succeeded only in making both face and hands equally dirty. So she gave it up and followed Will to the woodpile, where she sat and listened to his news of the village: Alyce Little was fat and bonny and had three teeth; the baker's wife kept her husband tied on a short rein to his ovens; Grommet Smith had married Aldon Figtree, understeward at the manor, a timid little man who called her "Mistress Figtree, my dear" and stayed mostly out of her way for fear of being swatted like a fly.

"How you be, Alyce?" Will asked when he had run out of gossip. "Why did you run?"

Alyce thought of what she might say—"That village did not suit me" or "The midwife was stingy and greedy and harsh" or "I found I did not care for babies"—but when her mouth opened, out came the story of her failure with Emma Blunt and how she discovered she was too stupid to be the midwife's apprentice.

"Bah, Alyce. I seen you with Tansy. You got guts and common sense. Just because you don't know everything don't mean you know nothing. Even

85

Jane Midwife herself don't know everything, though she think she do," Will said, winking at her with an eye as green as new grass and as friendly as a summer sky. Suddenly shy, Alyce ran back into the inn and the visit was over, though she remembered it again and again during the weeks that followed.

Before the month was out, another familiar face showed at the inn. One day when Alyce returned from gathering wood sorrel to make a sauce, there at the table was Jane Sharp, the midwife herself, in her starched wimple and second-best gown, deep in earnest conversation with Magister Reese.

Alyce's face grew hot and then as cold as bare feet in January; her throat tickled and her eyes stung as she imagined the midwife telling Magister Reese of the girl's stupidity, her incompetence, and her failure. Run away, she said to herself. Run away. But her shame was less than her curiosity—that and her desire not to leave Magister Reese hearing only the worst of her—so she stayed, hiding in the shadows of the room to listen without being seen.

Jennet pinched her and thrust a jug into her hands, so she began to move toward the table as slowly and silently as she could until she was close enough to hear: "And I brewed her some of my sage tea, unequaled for a woman likely to miscarry due to the slipperiness of her womb."

Jane Sharp was not then talking of Alyce but of herself—Alyce should have known—and Magister Reese was writing it all down in his great encyclopaedia, while the cat nibbled his cheese and bread.

Jane continued. "I myself use a tea of black alder bark and smut rye to stop excessive bleeding, but I have heard that rubies, either worn on the body or ground to a powder and taken in warm wine, do even better, if the woman is lucky enough to own rubies and rich enough to let them be ground into . . ."

She never even noticed Alyce as the girl refilled her mug. Alyce returned to the shadows. "Will Russet," she heard the midwife say to Magister Reese, "a boy from the village, tells me my apprentice is here at the inn. My former apprentice, might I say, for she ran away. You seen her here? Skinny girl with black curls and big sad eyes, afraid to say boo."

Before Magister Reese could say nay or yea, the midwife went on. "She was not as stupid as some I have had, and better company, but still perhaps her going was for the best. She was not what I needed."

"Because I failed," whispered Alyce in the shadows.

"Because she gave up," continued the midwife. "I need an apprentice who can do what I tell her, take what I give her, who can try and risk and fail and try again and not give up. Babies don't stop their borning because the midwife gives up." She landed her sharp glance on Magister Reese for a moment, drank off her ale in one long swig, and was gone.

# 14.
# The Manor

JUST BEFORE THE ROAD from the inn turns and makes for the village, there is a hidden path to the manor. Visitors use the main manor road, crossing through the gatehouse and past the apple trees and the stable. Some of the villagers know about the path, but few use it, for it passes too close to the dark woods. Alyce, in her comings and goings through the village, had come upon the path, although she had never before had need to follow it all the way up to the manor. Until one afternoon, when golden-yellow blossoms first appeared on the laburnum trees and Girtle the cow gave birth to her first calf, a sweet and sticky thing Alyce thought to call Rosebud, for she was as red as the hedgeroses near the village church.

As she watched Girtle nuzzle and suckle Rosebud and tuck her against her warm body to give the calf her warmth, Alyce was filled with a sudden longing to go to the boy Edward at the manor and see for herself that he was there, fed and dry and content. Mayhap he was unhappy and longing for her and she would bring him back to the inn and take care of him as Girtle did Rosebud. For days she thought about this, and the more she thought, the righter it seemed.

She imagined Edward's first sight of her at the manor. "Alyce, you have not forgot me," he would cry, throwing his arms about her waist. "Have you come to take me away? I pray you have, for I am desolate here without you and as well am starving and beaten and forced to sleep outside in the snow and no one cares for me." She would scoop the boy up in her arms and they would go together back to the inn and Alyce would take care of Edward and this would make her heart content.

All she needed was Edward and all would be well. She was certain of it. So one day when Jennet had gone to the market fair at Edenwick to buy a copper pot, a young pig, and a bit of lace for her best kirtle, and no guests but Magister Reese cluttered the table, Alyce put the cat in the stable so that he would not follow her and, the sun warming her wintry spirit, climbed to the manor on its gray-green hill.

Passing the village fields, she saw Roger Mustard and Thomas the Stutterer swinging their weed hooks and felt the familiar feelings in her chest and her throat, but turned her eyes away so she would not have to think about what she had had and what she had lost.

The manor was bustling in the sunshine. She went first to the barn, where the men were sharpening hoes and sickles in preparation for the summer hay cutting. "The boy Edward?" she asked a tall, red-nosed man. "The small boy who arrived after harvest to help with the threshing, is he still here?"

The man turned and looked at Alyce. "Forget this Edward, curly top. My name is Mat and I am six times the man he is. Climb up here on this hay bale and give me a warm, sticky kiss."

"My hair may be frizzled but my wits are not," Alyce responded. "Save your sticky kisses for your wife or your cow."

Alyce left the barn and went next to the smithy,

where the manor blacksmith and his apprentices were hammering lumps of iron into shoes for horses. "The boy Edward?" she asked again. Her answer was rude remarks, laughter, and kissing sounds from men too ill-tempered or too busy or too tired to care about the questions of a strange girl.

"The boy Edward?" Alyce asked the kitchen maid skinning a pig in the manor yard, the laundress boiling great kettles of goose fat for soap, the carpenters fashioning a coffin for Old Ned, who had died that morning. None answered. "Corpus bones!" said Alyce. "I might as well be asking the fence."

Finally she found her way to the shed that served as the manor kitchen and there found a cook who, judging from the words pouring forth from her mouth with none to listen, would not be reluctant to talk to Alyce.

"Please, ma'am," said Alyce, who had learned that *ma'am*s and *sirs* served her well even with cooks and stableboys when asking favors. "Please, ma'am, the boy Edward who came after harvest to help with the threshing, is he still here? Have you seen aught of him?"

"Ah, the lamb," the cook cooed, waving her

ladle at Alyce, "the little lamb. He be here. But too small he is to be swinging that great heavy flail about or wrestling with the oxen and ploughs and the taunting of the men, so I try to watch over him, the wee duckling, and find him simple tasks to do, suited for a small boy." The cook sat down, her face red from the heat and emotion and the boiling and stewing going on about her, took off one great leather shoe, and used it to fan her face. She peered closely at Alyce. "Surely then you be the sister he talks about, for you look just like him and could pass for twins." The cook muttered and crossed herself. "You not be twins?" she asked Alyce, peering closer. "I cannot abide twins."

"No, ma'am. We be not even brother and sister."

"Ah, never say that, sweet pudding, for you are as alike as two peas. Just so you are not twins."

"No, ma'am, not twins," answered Alyce again, wondering why twin cows such as Baldred and Billfrith should be such a joy and a boon while twin babies were ill-starred and unlucky.

"Well, then, my little turnip. Go find your brother in the hen house behind the barn, where I sent him to gather eggs for a parsley omelet. And

93

bring yourselves back here for a dinner of bread and bacon." The cook wiped her wet red face on her skirt, picked a struggling fly from the great pot of soup she was stirring, and began a new conversation with herself, for she found such talk interesting and hardly ever disagreed with what was said.

## 15.
# Edward

THE MANOR WAS GROWING QUIET, preparing
for evening and supper and bed. Alyce passed
men coming back from the fields, weed hooks and
hoes and rakes on their tired shoulders; dairymaids
washing out the churns, stopping every now and
then to lick the sweet butter off their fingers; shepherds bringing in the sheep for tomorrow's washing and shearing, the music of their pipes rising to
the wide blue sky and disappearing into the
silence.

Around the barn in the hen house she found
Edward, egg basket still empty, kneeling before the
chickens. "So then," he said to the largest and most
bad-tempered, "you be the king and you"—he
pointed to a small hen with speckled feathers—"be

the queen, for you look motherly and kind, and the rest of us will be knights and we will pretend we are about to have a great battle with the Scots but we don't mind for we are sure to be victorious."

At that, Edward looked up and saw Alyce watching him. "Alyce," he cried, leaping to his feet, the better to throw his arms about her waist. "Alyce, you have not forgot me." Alyce remembered her imaginings as the boy hugged her, and she smiled. It would be well.

"Come, Alyce, you can be a knight, too, and we will march north to the stable."

"Edward, I sent you here to work so you'd have food and warmth and a place to belong, and instead you're playing knights with the chickens. What be you thinking?" She tweaked Edward's nose and pulled a speckled feather from his hair. "Come, I'll help you find enough eggs to satisfy the cook, and then we will talk together."

"Alyce, what you be doing at the manor?"

"I came to see how you be, and good thing I did, for it seems you have not the wits of an oat. Your sister, indeed. What are these lies you have been telling the cook?"

"Not really lies, Alyce. I just wanted a sister, for

all Cook's other children have brothers and sisters. Have you come to take me away?"

Before Alyce could reassure him that she was there to rescue him and all would be well, he continued, "You haven't, have you, Alyce? For I am sore content here and mostly have enough to eat, and when Cook is cross with me I sleep with the chickens and pretend. No one chases me away and even Lord Arnulf knows my name."

So Alyce learned about the sometimes mighty distance between what one imagines and what is. She would not be bringing Edward back with her to make her heart content, but she knew she had not failed him, and she breathed a heavy sigh of sadness, disappointment, and relief. It felt so good that she did it again and again until her sighs turned to sobs and she cried her first crying right there in the hen house with Edward arming the chickens for battle. Edward patted her shoulders and hands and comforted her as well as a small boy could and cheered her by wiggling his loose front tooth.

On the way back to the kitchen Edward began a campaign to convince Alyce to stay the night and she agreed, though she knew Jennet would scold her for her absence, for she was not ready yet to completely abandon Edward and her rosy imaginings.

While they ate their bread-and-bacon supper, while Alyce helped Edward mound up straw in a corner of the kitchen, while she sat by watching for him to go to sleep, all the while Edward talked of life on the manor. He told her of the silken-robed lords and ladies who came for feasts and rode out to hunt and danced like autumn leaves in the candlelit great hall, of the visiting knights who clanked their swords against each other as they practiced in the school yard, of the masons who slapped mortar and bricks together to build a great new tower at the corner of the hall that looked to stretch near all the way to heaven. He described the excitement of buying and selling at the great autumn horse fair, the nervous preparations accompanying the arrival of some velvet-shod bishop or priest, and the thrill of watching the baron's men ride out to confront a huge maddened boar who had roamed too close to the village. And he complained at his lot, doing all the smallest tasks, not being allowed to help with the threshing and ploughing, being teased for being so little and frail and tied to Cook's skirts and fit for nothing but gathering eggs. Finally as his eyes looked near to closing, he said, "Tell me a story, Alyce."

"I don't know any stories."

"For sure you do. Everyone does."

"Well, Jennet told me that one night a visiting mayor fell out of bed, hit his head, and thought he was a cat, so he slept all night on the floor watching the mouseholes."

"That is no story, Alyce. Cook tells me stories. A story should have a hero and brave deeds."

"Well then, once there was a boy who for all he was so small and puny was brave enough to do what he must although he didn't like it and was sometimes teased. Is that a story?"

"Close enough, Alyce." And he closed his eyes.

When the moon shone through the misty clouds and two owls hooted in the manor yard, Edward and Alyce slept, each comforted by knowing the other was safe and warm and sheltered and not too very far away.

The next day being the day the woolly black-faced sheep were washed before shearing, Alyce and Edward ate their bread-and-beer breakfast down by the river to watch the great event.

Edward finished his breakfast first. "I'm still hungry, Alyce, and there is nothing about here to eat but grass. Do you know if grass is good for people to eat?"

"Try it."

He did. "It be good for exercising my teeth and making my mouth taste better, but it tastes like . . . grass, I would say."

"Then do not eat it."

"What is the best thing you ever ate, Alyce?"

"Hot soup on a cold day, I think."

"Once long ago a monk gave me a fig. It was a wonderful thing, Alyce, soft and sweet. After that I had nothing to eat for three days but the smell of the fig on my fingers. Are you ever going to finish that bread, Alyce?"

And Alyce gave him her bread, which is what Edward wanted and Alyce intended all along.

Part of the river had been dammed to form a washing pool. Men stood in the waist-deep water while the hairy shepherds, looking much like sheep themselves, drove the woolly beasts into the water to have their loose fleeces pulled off and then be scrubbed with the strong yellow soap. The river was noisy with the barking of dogs, the bleating of sheep, the calling and cursing of men, and the furious bawling of those lambs separated from their mothers. Edward soon took on the job of matching mothers and babies. He snatched up the bawling lambs and ran from mother to mother until he made up the right pair, whereupon they would knock him out of the way in their hurry to nuzzle each other.

As the day grew hotter the river looked cooler, and finally Alyce tucked her skirt up into her belt and waded in. The weary men were glad of another pair of hands and soon had Alyce helping. First she held the woolly black faces while they were scrubbed, but one old ewe took offense at Alyce's handling and, standing up with her front feet on Alyce's chest, pushed the girl into the water. Alyce, coughing and sputtering, traded jobs with the man who was lathering their backs. Fleeces clean, the sheep swam to the bank and scrambled out of the water, nimble as goats and hungry as pigs.

By midafternoon they were finished. While Edward and the shepherds drove the sheep to their pens across the field, Alyce stretched and wiped her wet hands on her wet skirt. What a wonder, she thought, looking at her hands. How white they were and how soft. The hours of strong soap and sudsy fleece had accomplished what years of cold water never had—her hands were really clean. There was no dirt between her fingers, around her nails, or ground into the lines on her palms. She sat back against a tree, held her hands up before her, and admired them. How clean they were. How white.

Suddenly she sat forward. Was the rest of her then that white and clean under all the dirt? Was her face white and clean? Was Will Russet right—was she even *pretty* under the dirt? There never had been one pretty thing about her, just skinny arms and big feet and dirt, but lately she had been told her hair was black and curly and her eyes big and sad and she was mayhap even pretty.

Alyce looked about. The washing was done and the sheep driven to the barn to dry off for tomorrow's shearing. The river was empty but for great chunks of the greasy yellow soap floating here and there. Alyce found a spot a bit upriver from the befouled washing pool, pulled off her clothes, and waded in. She rubbed her body with the yellow soap and a handful of sandy gravel until she tingled. Squatting down until the water reached her chin, she washed her hair and watched it float about her until she grew chilled.

Alyce stood up in the shallow water and looked at herself. Much cleaner, although a bit pink and wrinkled from her long soak. And pretty? Mayhap even that, for she had all her teeth and all her limbs, a face unmarked by pox or witchcraft, and perhaps, now, more of happiness and hope than of sadness in those big eyes that even the midwife had remarked on.

She washed her clothes, pulled them on still wet and drippy, and ran for the kitchen to dry a bit before the fire.

Too soon it was time to bid Edward good-bye. "Be assured I will not be far from here, and I promise to come back for Christmas and Easter and your saint's day. And to see when that front tooth grows in again." Edward grinned. He had enjoyed the day, done a man's job, and been carried home on the shoulders of a giant of a shepherd called Hal. He was satisfied with his place at the manor, the devotion of the cook, and the friendship of Alyce. He suddenly felt not so small.

Alyce gave him a hug and a smack and felt that tickling in her throat and stinging in her eyes that meant she might cry again, now she knew how to do it. She went down the path from the manor, stopping every few steps to turn and wave until finally the path curved and Edward was lost from sight and all she could see was the way ahead.

# 16.
# The Baby

ONE WARM EVENING CAME A STILLNESS as if the whole world were holding its breath. Thunderstorm, thought Alyce, as she hurried to fasten the wooden shutters over the windows before the skies opened.

Just then a party of riders rode into the inn yard—a prosperous-looking man wearing too much jewelry, a stout lady in some obvious discomfort, and their attendants, a man and woman sullen and none too bright looking. The man lifted the stout lady down and they hurried into the inn, leaving the boy Tam to put the horses away and see them dry and fed for the night.

Because they appeared important, Jennet herself bustled over to see to their needs.

"Supper, sir? Cold beef and the best bread in the county? A jug of ale or some Rhenish wine?"

"We want no food," said the prosperous-looking man.

"How then can I serve you?"

"In no way, madam, unless you be a priest, a magician, or a man of medicine. My wife is being devoured by a stomach worm."

The woman moaned a little and then let out a great cry that nearly drowned out the thunder crashing about them. Jennet crossed herself as the man swept platters and mugs off the big table and helped his wife lie down.

Snatching a mug of ale from John Dark, Jennet brought it to the wailing woman. She watched a moment and then laid her rosy hand on the woman's swollen belly. "In truth, sir, I think she is about to give you a child."

The man looked at Jennet with displeasure and dislike. "Get away with you, fool! My wife has been barren since the day of our marriage and breeds nothing but discontent. She has in truth grown stout of late, but that be herring pie and almond puddings. Having a child? Impossible!"

Jennet watched a few moments more. "Not only possible, sir, but soon."

The entire company looked then at the woman on the table, who was struggling to sit up and was pushing so hard her red face looked near to bursting.

"Impossible," said the man again, a little less confidently this time. "What should be done?"

The woman let out a bellow like a bull and John Dark hurried outside, preferring the rain to this.

"There is a midwife in the village some walk down that road. I will point your man the way," said Jennet.

So for a time the inn resounded with the rumble of the thunder, the cries of the laboring mother, and the useless clucking of the woman's husband.

Finally the manservant reappeared, as wet as water could make him. "I found the midwife's cottage where you told me," he said. "The midwife was not there and no fire is lit and it looks like some other child is making his way into the world tonight with the midwife to assist him. This one must make his own way."

All was noise and confusion as the woman pulled herself up again and commenced bellowing. Her husband gave her his ruby ring to hold. Jennet gave her ale. The manservant gave her a black look and went outside to join John Dark in the rain.

As night deepened, the woman's cries grew louder and louder. Jennet hustled and bustled, but she knew about brewing and baking and not babies, and all her bustle could not help. Magister Reese went out and returned, went out and returned, unable to help but reluctant to leave. Alyce stood watching from a place under the stairs, unwilling to be part of the scene, for the sounds and smells were all too familiar and spoke of her failure with Emma Blunt. She was kept from leaving altogether by her sympathy and compassion, and by a certain curiosity that compelled her to know what was happening and to what end and what might be done to finish or hasten or ease.

As the wails of the companions grew near as loud as those of the mother, Jennet threw them all outside—the woman attendant who shrieked more than she attended, the wailing husband, and Magister Reese, who then stood at the shuttered window, frantically paging through his Great Work looking for something to help and every now and then calling, "Jennet, you must find the bulb of a white lily" or "Virgins' hair and ant eggs!" or "An eagle-stone! Who has an eaglestone?"

Finally Jennet covered the moaning woman with her cloak, and, whispering "I can do no more. This baby will not come," slipped from the room.

Lightning lit up the room, empty but for Alyce under the stairs and the woman, in tears, in pain, in labor, and none to help. Alyce trembled. I should, she said to herself, but I cannot. I tried before and failed. You must, said herself back to her. None so stupid, said Magister Reese. You are nitwit, said Grommet Smith. Guts and common sense, said Will Russet. You gave up, said the midwife. "Help me," cried the woman on the table. "Keep still, all of you, and let me try," said Alyce, coming out from behind the ladder.

She got the woman to her feet and walked her around the room, stopping every now and then to pour some ale into her. She rubbed and oiled and pushed. She bade the woman sit and stand, kneel and lie down. She called on all those saints known to watch over mothers—Saint Margaret and Saint Giles and Saint Felicitas, and even Saint Loy, who protects horses, and Saint Anthony, who does the same for pigs, for she believed it would do no harm. She did every single thing she had seen the midwife do and even invented some of her own. As the thunderstorm passed and night prepared to yield to dawn, on a scarred wooden table that had seen more of pork pies and beer than babies, Alyce delivered a baby boy, with the black hair of his father and the red face of his mother.

Alyce had no basket of clean linen and ointments and herbs, so she tore a coarse thread from the hem of the woman's dress, tied the baby's cord, and cut it with a carving knife borrowed from the kitchen. Having no cumin or cecily for sealing the cord, she spat on her hand and rubbed the cut end.

Alyce then opened the door. "Here, sir," Alyce said, handing the baby to his father, "no stomach worm, but a loud and lusty boy."

His mother shouted from inside, "Stomach worm, bah! In truth I thought a dragon was eating my innards. Give the lout to me, I will teach him to give such trouble and pain to his mother." The stupefied father took the baby to his mother, who commenced scolding and berating the little fellow, all the while smoothing his black hair and caressing his little hands, until her scolding turned to cooing and his loud cries to gurgles, and mother and child fell asleep there on the inn table.

Alyce saw the man and his servants staring at her in awe. "It be a miracle," they whispered. "We have seen barren woman give birth, stomach worm transformed to innocent babe, dragon defeated by a girl who appeared from nowhere!"

The man spoke to Alyce. "Good miss, be you an angel or a saint?"

Alyce stared at him. "An angel? I be no angel."

"Then it is saint you are!" he cried, and all about fell to their knees in wonder.

"No," Alyce repeated. "No saint, no angel. Corpus bones, I but delivered a child. Your wife never had a stomach worm."

But the man and the servants, still on their knees before her, prayed and thanked her for the cure of their mistress and the miracle of the baby, and while she was at it, the female servant asked for a warm cloak for winter and that the wart should fall off her chin.

Alyce pushed past them and stepped out into the warm night. The moon was as round and as white as a new cheese. On a bench beneath the old oak sat John Dark and Magister Reese, sharing a mug of ale. Magister Reese winked at her and smiled. Alyce smiled back. And then she laughed, a true laugh that came from deep in her gut, rushed out her mouth, and rang through the clear night air. And that was the true miracle that night, the first of June—the month, as Magister Reese could have told her, named for Juno, the Roman goddess of the moon, of women, and of childbirth.

# 17.

# The Midwife's Apprentice

JUNE BURST INTO BLOOM—daisies, larkspur, meadowsweet and thyme, foxglove and thimbleberry, purple thistle flowers, and yellow whorls of blooming fennel. Alyce sat in the meadow and thought. The rich merchant and his wife wished to take her back with them to Salisbury to care for their son and mayhap perform more miracles; he spoke temptingly of new shoes and a shrine. Magister Reese was leaving the inn to return to the lodgings in Oxford he shared with his widowed sister and wished to employ Alyce: "My sister grows older and needs more care than I can give her, and I think mayhap Oxford would please you." Alyce liked being invited, but Jennet scowled and moped, unwilling to lose a willing worker but even sadder to see the last of the girl herself, and finally offered Alyce a penny every now and then if she would agree to stay.

As she chewed on a grass, Alyce smiled. From someone who had no place in the world, she had suddenly become someone with a surfeit of places. She closed her eyes and continued to chew. What to do? What do I want? she asked herself in the manner she had learned from Magister Reese, who thought it fitting for even an inn girl to want.

In her mind she saw Magister Reese's spotted face and kind eyes, heard Jennet's merry voice, and smelled the rich perfumed robes of the merchant from Salisbury. She felt again the vigorous, squirming, wonderful aliveness of the merchant's son as he wriggled into her hands. She heard the joyful chatter of birds building their nests in the thatch of the church, saw the triumph on the face of the midwife as she coaxed a reluctant baby into life, remembered the silky feel of Tansy's newborn calves and the sticky softness of the baby called Alyce Little.

"Of course," she whispered, eyes opening wide. "Of course." She was not an inn girl or a nursery maid or a companion to old women. She was a midwife's apprentice with a newborn hope of being someday a midwife herself. She had much still to learn, and she knew a place where she could learn it, cold and difficult and unwelcoming as that place might be. That was her place in this world for right now, and though her belly would likely never be full, her heart was content.

That night she dreamt she gave birth to a baby who gave birth to a baby and so on and so on until morning.

Early in the day she saw the merchant and his family off to Salisbury, bid farewell to Magister Reese and sent her respects to his sister, hugged Jennet, and set off for the village, comb and soap and page from a great and holy book tucked in her bodice and orange cat at her heels.

Not too long after this the inn, which had been known simply as John Dark's place, came to be called The Cat and Cheese, marked by a great hanging sign of an orange cat with a morsel of cheese in his paw. Within a few years no one remembered why, but so it is called to this day.

As she swung along the village road, Alyce, with good feelings tumbling about inside her, hummed and then tra-la-ed and then sang, as loud and clear as a swan. Some of the words were without meaning, others just sounded right, but some words came from deep inside her and told how she felt about life and hope and the road ahead.

"Come summer, come flowers, come sun," sang Alyce.

"Purr," sang the cat.

Alyce knocked at the midwife's door, surprised at how the French roses had grown since last she was there.

"Jane, I am back," she said to the frowning midwife. "I be a fine midwife's apprentice now. I know about babies and birthing, singing songs and cooking chickens, crying and laughing and reading."

"Is that all?" asked Jane.

"Are these not excellent things for a midwife's apprentice to know?"

"They are indeed, but is that all?"

"That is all and I am here."

But Jane would not have her. Alyce stood before the cottage, eyes stinging and heart sore. She had not thought about this, had thought no further than knocking on Jane's door and being welcomed. But there it was. Jane would not have her. And before morning turned to afternoon and the morning glories turned their faces from the sun, Alyce, in despair and confusion, turned from the village, fearful that each step would take her once again over that invisible line that separated the village from the rest of the world.

But the cat would not.

"I know you do not wish to leave, cat. Nor do I. But there is no place for me here. I tried to come back but failed. She will not have me."

Purr laid himself down, tucked his front paws under the white spot on his chest, and looked at her with his gooseberry eyes.

"What then should I do?" Alyce sat down and listened to the humming of the bees and the purring of the cat. Suddenly she leapt to her feet. "Corpus bones, you are right, cat! Jane herself told me what she needed."

Alyce turned back again for the cottage, gathering comfrey leaves and raspberries and the tiny wild strawberries in her skirt as she went. She marched up to the midwife's door and knocked firmly.

"Jane Sharp! It is I, Alyce, your apprentice. I have come back. And if you do not let me in, I will try again and again. I can do what you tell me and take what you give me, and I know how to try and risk and fail and try again and not give up. I will not go away."

The door opened. Alyce went in. And the cat went with her.

# Author's Note

As long as there has been a woman giving birth and another to help her, there have been midwives. In developed countries today, most births take place in hospitals attended by doctors. This is not so throughout the world and certainly was not true in the past. Until the twentieth century, the overwhelming majority of women giving birth did so at home attended by other women.

The woman who made a profession of helping women in labor was called a midwife, from Middle English words meaning "with woman." Sometimes the midwife was the oldest woman in the village or the one who had the most children. Sometimes a woman could get no other work, because she was poor or ignorant or dirty, so she hired herself out as midwife for women who could afford no other help. Lucky women were attended by a midwife with a deep commitment, skill, and training through experience or apprenticeship, and with patience, judgment, and clean hands.

Different times and different places saw midwives differently, as almost-doctors or as almost-witches. In medieval England, midwifery was a less than honorable profession, mostly because it was practiced by and on women. Midwives worked unsupervised and unregulated into the sixteenth century, when Henry VIII's efforts to centralize and supervise the medical profession resulted in the registration and regulation of midwives.

Medieval midwifery was a combination of common sense, herbal knowledge, and superstition, passed from woman to woman through oral tradition and apprenticeship. Things were done the way they had long been done, with little innovation or progress. This "women's knowledge" was considered reliable and valuable, as illustrated in this book by the inclusion of Jane Sharp's information in Magister Reese's great encyclopaedia.

Midwives in general used their common sense to help the woman in labor relax, to comfort and soothe her physically and emotionally, to call on all the natural and magical agents at their disposal, and to assess when things were going badly. Some, like Jane Sharp, were experienced enough to know when and how to interfere. Others just tormented the struggling woman with their meddling. Medieval common sense knew nothing of germs, little of anatomy, and all too much of magic and superstition.

Herbs were the only medicines available to the medieval midwife. They were selected, picked, dried, and prepared according to ancient recipes and rituals, which took into consideration where and when the herbs were picked, what their leaves or flowers looked or tasted like, and the influence of the ruling planets. Plants under the influence of Mars, used to treat complaints of organs under the influence of Mars, were usually ineffective, as were those given to stanch blood or increase milk because their flowers looked like drops of blood or milk. But many herbs actually were effective, such as birthwort for inducing contractions, lady's mantle to stop bleeding, wormwood to relieve pain, and hops for their calming effect. The derivatives of some herbs used by midwives are used in medicine today: belladonna to calm spasms and cramps, smut rye to stimulate uterine contractions, henbane and poppy for relief from pain.

Superstitions included the use of relics, water from holy wells, charms, and magic words. Snail jelly for childbirth fever and eel liver to ease labor were considered useful, as were precious stones—

notably jasper, emerald, and ruby—either held in the mother's hand or crushed into powder and mixed in wine. If these practices helped, it was not through magical intervention, but because of the calming and strengthening effect of the midwife and mother's faith in their efficacy.

No matter how skillful and conscientious she was, a midwife was really only of help in a normal delivery. No amount of magic stones or herbal syrups could correct a serious problem, such as a woman's small or deformed pelvis or a child in a position making passage through the birth canal impossible. Many mothers and children died in childbirth during the Middle Ages, the result of poor nutrition and care, the number of unskilled midwives, and the inadequate state of medical knowledge.

With the increased participation of doctors in the birth process, midwives fell into disrepute, but since the 1960s, there has been renewed interest in midwifery in this country and elsewhere. The midwifery profession is now regulated, and individual midwives are licensed. Today's midwives offer women much more than clean hands, magic stones, and snail jelly. Midwives can be men or women;

some are nurses also; some deliver babies at home and others in hospitals. In France, a midwife is *sage femme*, wise woman; in Denmark, *jordemoder*, earth mother; among Yiddish-speaking Jews, *vartsfroy*, waiting woman; in Hawaii, *pale keiki*, protector of the child. Throughout the world midwifery continues to exist alongside medicine for women who choose to continue the tradition.

# History comes alive!

# The best of Mary Downing Hahn

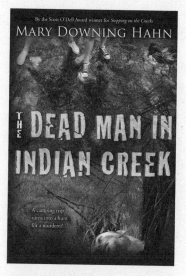

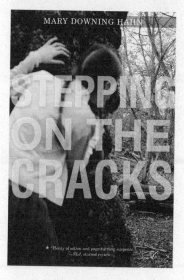

Winner of the Scott O'Dell
Book Award